Dear Bre

Thanks f

me up in the mornings!

Weekender

Weekender

Roland Tye

Comely Bank Publishing

This edition published 2016 by Comely Bank Publishing

Cover design by Natalie Schupfer and Joseph White

Cover photo by Kacper Rogala

Text printed in Garamond by 4Edge

ISBN: 978-0-9573521-8-6

A CIP catalogue record for this book is available from the British Library

Dedicated to Tenteleni

Born in the winter of discontent, Roland Tye has spent most of his life in Edinburgh and Dundee. There was a brief sojourn to study in The Netherlands but he can't remember very much about it now.

Weekender is his first novel.

Friday

Saturday

Sunday

Monday

Friday

It was a dull, dreary October afternoon just shy of the new Millennium. The sort of day the island suffered continually from August through to April. In the darkening sky, heavy clouds blocked out all natural light, their listless tone matching that of the grey tenements they shrouded. The rain was falling and had been all day.

In a soulless office block on the edge of town a young man called Anthony fed paper into a bulky photocopier. Every so often the hulk of plastic would produce a mangled cry, forcing Anthony to dig around in its guts to retrieve creased parchment.

His colleague said that the number of paper jams is directly proportional to the urgency multiplied by the importance of the work you are copying, which in turn is directly related to the number of people who also need to use the photocopier. On that basis, his was the most urgent and important photocopying job of all time and everyone else in the building wanted to use the precious machine.

He was hungry, the bland cheese sandwich he'd eaten at lunch not nearly enough. He wanted to nip to the vending machine for some chocolate but that would mean abandoning the photocopier and the aforementioned rule meant it was guaranteed that someone else would nab it in his absence. The other photocopier on his floor was broken, had been all week, and Anthony had more than a hundred documents still to copy before the end of the day.

Failure would result in a roasting from his supervisor, and kept Anthony at his post as his stomach growled. The thought of the slimy reptile's ugly, reddening face exploding millimetres from

Anthony's. The stench of his fag-and-coffee breath. The sodden patches under his armpits as his hands flailed above this head. Flecks of spittle shooting from his lips as he swore blue murder, then an irate call to the agency swiftly followed by Anthony's marching orders. It had happened to Jason only last week, something minor not even his fault. Stevie the month before that. Again totally undeserved. All the temps danced on eggshells and Anthony needed to maintain the nimble abilities of a ballerina at all times. No mistakes. No cock-ups. Others were queueing up behind him to take his place.

It was Friday and the weekend was on its way. A time of fun and frivolity. A time for the forbidden. Anthony had plans, some concrete, others still not fully formed. As he continued his mechanical interactions, he mulled over what was to unfold. There was a night out on Saturday. Drinking followed by more drinking. The lion's share of his weekly pay would evaporate. A kick-about in Inverleith on Sunday. Hungover no doubt. He'd either play a blinder or a stinker. Then Sunday lunch with the extended family. Great food. Boring chat. Tonight, however, was still a blank canvas. One to ponder between now and home time.

With more than fifty copies still to do, the photocopier emitted a hopeless sigh and seized up completely. Not a paper jam this time. Something much more serious. Perhaps fatal. The infernal photocopier sat useless and dormant.

He looked up at the clock and sighed. His time was yet to come.

James Urquhart

For James Urquhart the weekend had started early. With a hamburger in one hand and a can of lager in the other, he planned the rest of the afternoon from the comfort of his modest saloon car. He felt pretty pleased with himself, having managed to hoodwink the corporation out of a few precious hours by conniving a meeting that did not exist. He was now able to execute what his mind had been feverishly deliberating for some time. Deep in the bowels of a multi-storey car park, hidden from the prying eyes of the rest of the world, he plotted and schemed.

A few chomps and slurps later, the meal was gone. Heartburn set in and he fished in the glove compartment for some Rennies. He crunched down on two of the chalky pills and then immediately lit a Rothman, wheezing down the clingy smoke and blowing it out with an exasperated cough. He always choked on the first draw these days. One of life's few pleasures was becoming a drag.

Plumes of blue soon filled the car and he wound down the window to alleviate himself from the acrid smog. The breeze was nippy yet refreshing and he began to breathe more easily. His thoughts returned to the matter at hand.

There was still time to reverse. To backtrack. There always was. But James Urquhart had neither the will nor the inclination to make that choice. Instead, his body began to tingle with that excited and forbidden expectation. The sensation of immorality prickled under his skin. As his palms sweated, his trousers bulged. With every racing thought blood rushed faster and faster through his body. All in one direction.

Steadying himself, he opened the black briefcase sitting next to him and reached inside. As his sticky hands caressed the rough newsprint, his reddening face swivelled quickly and anxiously from side to side. James Urquhart was not a regular *Sport* reader. He was very firmly a *Daily Mail* man. But on occasions such as these only the *Sport* would do.

He eagerly thumbed his way to the classifieds. They boasted a plethora of minute phone numbers, each prefixed by an abbreviated description –

Ggow'O'forU

AbdnKinky

*NW18-55

GgowDom/Sub

EdinMature44DD

Manc Stockings*A

The list seemed endless, the selection infinite. Only a few of the numbers were applicable, however, and he mentally discarded the rest as he scanned the mass of black and white for the magical four letters – EDIN. There were those he recognised from past encounters and some he'd called before but hadn't frequented. Others were new and therefore exciting. An unknown quantity.

In total there were fourteen local numbers, all of which he carefully ringed with a chewed biro. Three specialised exclusively in domination. Not his thing. Another two cited a 'mature lady'. This was code for a fifty-something old boot, haggard and worn, with yellow teeth, wrinkly skin and make-up so thick it had most likely been applied with a trowel. That was certainly not his thing. James Urquhart liked them young and preferably innocent. The latter was hardly likely, however. Not in these particular circles.

That left nine dens of iniquity. These were –

SexyTina
24U
Heaven/Hell
All Fantasies
BlondKaren
Kinky n Rude
PrivDiscreet
New Central
LesboDuo

James Urquhart's gleaming eyes darted from one number to the next. Which to phone first?

He plumped for 'All Fantasies', mainly because he had visited there before and knew what to expect. This call would be the icebreaker. Nice and easy. Still, he couldn't bring himself to dial in the numbers on the mobile phone that was now in his greasy, trembling hand. Twice he started to dial and then cancelled. He eventually completed the process, only to be offended by the shrill whine of an engaged tone. He let out a grumble. Best try another.

0…1…3…then he stopped. Guilt reared its unwelcome head as thoughts of work, of his family, of responsibility and decency momentarily gripped him. He shook them aside and began to dial the first number again. The icebreaker.

It rang.

"Hello, how may I help you?"

The business-like voice was instantly recognisable to James Urquhart. He had heard it many times before. It was the same lady who always answered the phone and greeted him at the door. The madam.

He paused before responding, the familiar routine taking him by surprise as it always did.

"Ah…yes…hello…could you give me some details please?"

He always asked the same question in the same business-like way. The lady at the other end surely recognised him but still enquired "Have you been before, sir?"

"Yes, yes, I have," he stammered uncertainly. James Urquhart had been many times before. Too many times.

"I see, well, today we have our mature lady, Samantha."

His heart sank.

"And our blond girl, Tracy."

His interest revived.

"Samantha has long auburn hair."

Ginger.

"Is very buxom, with a fabulous, voluptuous figure."

Fat.

"And she specialises in all levels."

On drugs.

"Tracy is our gorgeous twenty three year old. She has short blond hair, lovely long legs, an all-over body tan, and beautiful green eyes. She specialises in oral without, watersports and domination."

Possibly.

"Would you be interested in paying us a visit?"

Her voice was prim and proper yet friendly. Inviting in a grandmotherly kind of way.

"What time do you close at?" asked James Urquhart, knowing full well it was about seven o'clock.

"About seven o'clock?"

"Right... okay... I'll think about it"

"Thank you. Goodbye."

And that was that. First mission accomplished. The blonde sounded like a decent option. One to remember. He would try a few more and then reach a decision.

He went for 'Sexy Tina' next. A new number. Again it took him an eternity to punch in the numbers.

It rang.

The phone had one of those bizarre dialling tones that echoed as though it were being monitored by the authorities. Perhaps it was.

"Hello?" came the irritated voice of a young woman.

"Ah...hello...could you give me some details please?"

"Have you been before?" asked the woman suspiciously.

"No...no I haven't."

"Right, well we're a private flat in the New Town. Do you know where that is?"

"Yes."

"Okay. It's ten pounds for your massage and between thirty and sixty after that." She then stopped her spiel, believing she had divulged ample information. There was a hint of anger in her voice.

James Urquhart hated these calls. They were both trying and embarrassing. It was as though he were being accused of something. He could only reason that she had received a number of crank calls earlier in the day and was therefore being stroppy to the point of obstruction.

"Who's the girl?"

"It's the same girl every day – Tina."

Her whole demeanour suggested they'd had this conversation before, which they hadn't.

"And what's she like?" he asked. More aggressively.

She sighed. "Mid twenties. Slim. Black hair."

"What time are you open till?"

"Nine."

James Urquhart took a mental note never to phone that number again, took a deep breath and contemplated his next move.

The small luminous green hand on the dashboard clock was nudging quarter past two. He had to be home by six. Just to keep up appearances. He doubted he'd be able to beat the rush hour traffic, which would shunt and stop its way infuriatingly to suburbia. That, and the inherent guilt in the aftermath, would put him in a foul mood for dinner. He certainly didn't want that. Not with all the arguing that had been going on recently. Then there was his pledge of a weekend fishing trip up north with wee Jimmy. He'd be irritable the whole time and wee Jimmy had some mouth on him. The last thing he wanted was to lose his temper and smack him again. Best to leave it for now. Ignore the urges just this once. There was always next week. And the week after that.

And yet he couldn't shake that nagging in the back of his head. The numbers on the page cavorted before him like topless dancers, each one a gateway to a secret, forbidden world. Each one an unknown, unseen chamber, hidden within the city. In a desert of normality these were oases of enjoyment seen only by those who knew where to look. James Urquhart knew.

He pressed the green call button once more, this time choosing '24U'. Another new number.

Another engaged tone.

"Fuck sake!"

He pressed redial. This time it rang.

"Hello…?"

The voice at the other end was shy. Almost nervous. He gave her his catchphrase question.

"Sure," she replied with a little more certainty. She sounded relatively inexperienced. This pleased him. He always liked to be in control, even with the receptionist.

"We're a private and discreet flat based just off Morrison Street."

"I see."

"We have two girls working today."

"Hmmm."

"Would you like me to describe them for you?" she asked somewhat saucily. More relaxed.

"Please!"

"The first is Natalie, she's our stunning brunette. She's twenty two with beautiful shoulder length brown hair, a gorgeous figure and lovely long legs that go on forever. Truly a stunner!"

The woman was in full flow now.

"The other girl we have on today is our teenager, Cindy."

James Urquhart's eyes lit up.

"She's eighteen, has a petite figure with long, straight blonde hair, an all-over body tan, and baby blue eyes to die for! Both girls are very experienced and cater for a wide range of fantasies! Would you be interested in making an appointment for this afternoon, sir?"

"What are the prices?"

"Forty to sixty all inclusive."

Still feeling his way around what he really wanted to say, James Urquhart asked "And what sort of facilities do you have?"

"Everything. TV, video, uniforms, toys. The lot!"

"Is it possible to have a two-girl?"

"One hundred and forty for a full show and personal service from both girls," was the response. "And they do everything – you won't be disappointed!"

"Right… okay."

Then for the crunch. The most awkward of all questions.

"Do either of them… em… specialise in… um… anything?"

"Did you have anything particular in mind?"

"Well… em… I'm not sure."

Anal!

"Do they do… em… oh… I don't know."

Anal!

"Like… em… domination or…"

Anal!

"Greek?"

"Natalie specialises in domination. Both do anal."

Bingo!

"And how much is that?"

"Which?"

"Greek."

"Anal sex is eighty pounds, sir!"

Her frankness dragged another blush from his sagging cheeks. He booked an appointment at four and hung up. Sweat dripped from his phone.

He made the short drive to his rendezvous and parked up. Sheltered in his car from the incessant rain, and still with plenty of time to spare, James Urquhart psyched himself up. What happened now depended very much on him. This would be a battle of will and of wits. A test of his nerves.

In such transactions the woman held all the cards. She wanted his money and, once paid, she wanted rid of him. She would use every trick in the book to bring him to ejaculation as quickly as possible and then send him on his way. For James Urquhart, these sojourns into the realms of fantasy were not for good sex. They were for power. Imaginary, momentary power, but for power nonetheless. That was why he preferred his girls young and inexperienced. So he could dominate them. An old hand would control him and ultimately leave him dissatisfied.

He reflected over and over again on the need to be strong and forthright. To be powerful was the key that would unlock the door to his perfect fantasy. He imagined himself barking orders at her, dominant and threatening, trying to seize back the power life had stolen from him.

"Get on your knees!"

"Suck it!"

"You fucking slut!"

It was time.

The entrance to paradise was hardly salubrious. A back-to-front swastika had been carved into the door. At its base were sinister black footmarks and dents to match. The intercom was old and shabby; two of the buzzers were missing, their wires hanging out in a straggled mess. His buzzer was there, however, and he pressed it tentatively.

Then a pause of anticipation. His heart pounded.

"Hello?" came the receptionist's voice.

"Hi…em…it's Peter."

James Urquhart preferred anonymity to intimacy and used his father's name on such occasions.

"Come on up. It's the second floor," came an inviting reply.

A tinny ring signalled admission and he pushed hard on the door. After an uncertain hiatus it opened with a jolt, almost causing him to trip up.

"Fuck sake!"

As he made his way up the stairs, his mind pondered a series of as yet unanswered questions.

Would she be attractive?

Would she give him short shrift or welcome him with open arms and legs?

Would she perform oral with or without a condom?

Would she play his kinky games or just lie there silent and indignant?

Soon all would be revealed.

The door to the parlour was slightly ajar, its safety chain in place. A single blue eye peered curiously through the crack. It surveyed James Urquhart. The door then opened quickly and a middle-aged woman hurried him inside.

The flat was smartly furnished but very clinical. It lacked the lived-in touches a real home possessed. This was a place of business. Nothing more.

His hostess led James Urquhart into a neat, functional kitchen/living room. Two smallish couches and an uncomfortable looking armchair surrounded a small television set. In the centre of the room was a glass coffee table; on its surface a burgeoning ashtray, twenty Regal and a further two crushed packs, as well as a collection of glossy women's magazines. The worktops at the back of the room were eerily sterile and bare save a kettle, some coffee cups and a bunch of fake plastic flowers floating in a garish orange plastic vase. A tacky pink wall-clock slowly ticked by above the silent drone of the muted television.

Sitting on the end of one of the couches was a woman reading the *Daily Record*. The cheap nylon dress she was wearing fell woefully short of covering her pale white thighs and drooping breasts. Her hair was dark and greasy, and worn in a nasty crinkled perm. Her pinched face was coated in thick, bright red lipstick and bruised purple eyeliner. Her eyes were cold, dull and distant. In her right hand was a cigarette, which looked as though it had been permanently welded there years ago.

"This is Natalie, one of our girls," explained the

receptionist politely.

Natalie momentarily glanced in James Urquhart's general direction, flashed him a fake smile, took a long drag on her cigarette and then returned to reading her comic.

"Please, take a seat," offered the still smiling receptionist.

He chose the armchair rather than sit beside either woman. Embarrassingly, his ample form squeezed its way uncomfortably between the arms until he was sandwiched like a fat slice of ham. Just a few years ago he would have slipped easily into it. He stared avidly at a silent game-show, trying not to look around or make eye contact.

"Our other girl, Cindy, is busy at the moment, but she'll be out in a few minutes. Would you like a cup of tea?"

"Em... no... no thank you." He almost stammered as he spoke. He hated this part. He just wanted to get on with it.

"Actually, could I possibly use your bathroom?"

"Certainly. If you'd just like to come this way."

Clutching his briefcase, James Urquhart was led into the hall and directed towards a small shower-room. He pulled over the bolt on the door with great relief. Loosening his tie, he cleansed his brow with plenty of liquid soap and hot water. Excitement mounting, he opened the briefcase and produced his magazine. Masturbation immediately prior to the event was imperative if he was to avoid a premature end.

Gazing at the vacant models, their legs spread, knickers round their ankles, soon brought him off.

A few strokes were all he required. After the initial, wonderful climax, he shamefully wiped away the sticky mess with a wad of toilet paper. Feeling hollow and empty, he no longer had the stomach for what he was about to do. By the time he had pulled his trousers up and returned to the living room, however, it was back on the agenda. The shame only ever lasted a few, painful, intense seconds.

He positioned himself awkwardly in the armchair once more, his eyes fixated on the screen. The other girl still hadn't arrived. He began to feel decidedly hot.

"Sure you wouldn't like a cup of tea?" she asked sweetly.

"No…really."

As he muttered, noises could be heard from next door; faint chattering, a woman's laugh, then a handle being turned, a door opening, and, finally, footsteps. It was finally time. His heart fluttered.

Worried that she might have been worse than the other woman, his fears were soon allayed. The girl in question was petite and attractive enough. Alluring in a sleazy, common way. The way he liked. She wore the sort of body-hugging black leather dress and knee-high boots favoured by such professionals. Her skin was pale and her hair dyed a poor blonde but this didn't particularly bother James Urquhart. She was neither fat nor ugly and most importantly, she looked young.

"Peter, this is Cindy."

He smiled meekly and was greeted by another false grin.

"So, which girl would you like? Or would you like

both?" The receptionist raised an eyebrow as both girls looked vacantly in front of them, completely disinterested. Cindy was now seated and sucking on a fresh cigarette.

"Em…I'd like to go with Cindy, please," he answered, looking uncertainly in her direction.

"Cindy?" enquired the now standing receptionist. She made it seem more of a question than the order it actually was.

"Sure."

Another fake smile brandished, she extinguished her cigarette and they departed to the boudoir.

Dimly lit in purple neon, the walls were blood red, one covered almost entirely by an enormous mirror. A king-size bed filled most of the room. Soft pillows, needlessly frilly sheets and a mock leopard skin rug attracted with a mixture of comfort and sleaze. Facing the bed on an old dresser was a large television and video recorder. Hanging on one wall was a collection of uniforms including that of a nurse, a schoolgirl, and a maid. Rubber suits, gimp masks, restraints and dildos were all accounted for. On one wall several cut-outs of naked women from adult publications were pinned up for the gentleman's benefit. By the bed was a table displaying a selection of condoms. The room was scented with a mixture of talc, oil and rubber, and underfoot was a plush black carpet. It was, without doubt, the forbidden chamber of sin he'd hoped for.

"Where you from?" came the girl's first inquiry. She had an English accent, which pleased James Urquhart no end. Female Scottish voices reminded him of his wife.

"Em…I'm from Edinburgh."

"Have you been working today?"

"Em…aye."

"What do you do?"

James Urquhart didn't like being questioned, particularly by women of her ilk, and muttered something about working in an office. He might engage in conversation afterwards but for now he simply wanted to satiate the demons. This she realised and cut the chitchat.

"Would you like to get undressed and I'll give you a massage?"

He nodded and began to strip self-consciously, ashamed of his recently expanding body. She paid no attention as his belly popped out and his pimply behind was bared. Naked, he lay face down on the bed and his insecurities melted away. She sat across his back, the heat from her crotch arousing him as it warmed the base of his spine. The slick caressing of his shoulders did likewise.

"Mmmmm!"

After a few blissful minutes, the fretting began. James Urquhart found it difficult to initiate sex, even with prostitutes, and both of them knew that she could carry on doing this for ten minutes or more. This would cut into his real fun. He wanted to take control, get things moving, but instead he just lay there, his mind in limbo.

Thankfully her caresses soon got lower, her palms spreading out over his large body, greasing his skin. Deftly, her hands reached under his flabby stomach, tantalising his genitals with little flicks of her fingers.

"So, is there anything else I can do for you?" she ventured suggestively.

"What do you do?" he asked, as deadpan as he could.

"Well, it's forty for hand relief, forty five for oral, fifty for sex, and sixty for everything."

"…And…em…do you do anything else?" he fished hesitantly.

"What're you after?"

"Em…well…the woman on the phone said you did…em…Greek," his voiced tailed off to a pathetic squeak.

"So, you want to fuck me up the arse?"

She looked directly at him in the mirror. A cat-like grin edged across her face.

"Em… yes!"

"Alright. That's eighty."

Relieved, James Urquhart produced his wallet from the trousers lying on the floor and stuffed a wad of crinkled notes into her palm. She counted them judiciously before placing them on the table by the bed.

"Now, how do you want me? Would you like me to dress up?" she asked, now in a far friendlier manner, and nodded towards the uniforms.

He studied the wall, quickly settling for the school uniform. Without ceremony she dropped her dress, revealing a lack of underwear, causing his manhood to twitch. Moments later she was transformed into his ideal fantasy. She was exactly what he had been dreaming of all afternoon – a naughty schoolgirl who did everything. The demons muttered their satisfaction.

James Urquhart lay on the bed, a serene peace now enveloping him as she went to work on his nether regions. The woman was certainly good at her job. Between slurps and ice cream licks she whispered jailbait pillow talk.

"You're a lot older than me... Please don't tell my parents about this."

He tried to get involved but was unable to participate in the very game he had initiated and paid for. Instead he gasped and moaned, desperately trying not to come as he watched her head bob up and down on his length in the mirror. As she ran her tongue from the tip of his erection to the base of his testicles, a finger cheekily tickled his anus.

She quickly and expertly rolled a sheath down his penis using her lips. A small tube of lubricant was used to grease his erection and her behind. The sensation made him wriggle.

Having briefly departed from his fantasy, she returned to being his naughty little schoolgirl. Playing cute and coy, she lay on her hands and knees in front of him, lifted up her skirt and spread her cheeks. Her anus stared back at him invitingly as he coarsely grabbed her firm buttocks.

"Please be gentle. It's my first time..."

The demons roared their approval.

After some uncomfortable pushing, more lubricant and some help from her, he was inside her. It felt tight. Constrictive. Exquisitely sore. He had no idea how it felt for her. He didn't care. In fact, he did. He hoped it hurt.

He studied her in the mirror, lapping up the pained expression on her face, her low, dull moaning causing him to push harder, getting further and deeper with each stroke. After a while she became accustomed to him, the process now smoother and easier. Her mood changed. Discomfort turned to boredom as she waited dutifully for him to have his fill, only sporadically becoming the fantasy he wanted.

He was off somewhere else. In dreamland. He slapped her backside and bawled obscenities in response to her mock adolescent murmurs.

"Ooh, it's really sore! I shouldn't be doing this…"

"Take it you little slut!" he grunted. "You fuckin' bitch, take my cock!"

And so on.

Then, all of a sudden and without warning, it happened. His mind drifted somewhere else. Just for a second. He was at half-mast before he knew it. He grabbed desperately at her body with his grubby fingers as his brain dug up every sexual thought it could unearth. Anything to keep it going. But there was no response. The condom shrivelled up around his penis, forcing him out of her. In vain he tried to force his way back.

To no avail.

"Shall I finish you by hand?"

He nodded mournfully.

Squeezing on cold oil, he writhed as she grabbed his penis and pulled hard. After a few strokes a semi-erection emerged.

"Come on, show me your spunk," she cried, winking as she brought him off.

He soon came over her hand, releasing a cry

more of pain and relief than of pleasure. James Urquhart hurriedly dressed and departed without saying a word.

Miss Richards

The bed sheets were dirty and would need a thorough wash. More of a problem was the cuff of the school shirt, which was covered in semen. There were other sheets but no shirts.

Calling this woman Cindy would be pointless, the name merely being a point of reference she had randomly been designated in her latest role. 'Cindy's' real name had been lost long ago. Irrelevant now, she simply called herself what she pleased. Only her surname – Richards – linked this young woman to a past she'd rather forget.

As a child, Miss Richards was weaned on a diet of fear. The knot of dread was a perpetual stone in the pit of her stomach. Fear was always there. Fear and violence. And Daddy.

At home her father's insidious presence could be felt everywhere, from the smell of the bathroom towels to the sound of the racing commentary on the radio. He was omnipotent, his drunken hatred saturating the atmosphere, poisoning the very air she breathed. The violence had been constant. Routine.

Her mother was a hopeless wretch of a woman. Less than five foot tall, waif-like and barely literate, she had fallen into a loveless relationship, become burdened with child, and then binged on painkillers to blot out the circumstances in which she found herself. She was unable to care for her daughter and too weak to protect her. At the age of fourteen Miss Richards found her swinging from a bed sheet. She ran away the same afternoon.

Predictably, Miss Richards made her way south to

the bright lights of London, the destination for a thousand broken dreams. She had never before left the town she had once called home. Except once on a day trip to Scarborough. London was something on television. Not real. Yet there she was, walking the city's streets, no idea of what to do or where to go.

There were people everywhere. Walking, running, shouting, laughing. So many people and of so many types. Every colour under the sun. Wherever Miss Richards looked she saw something new and different, and therefore exotic. The shops, the restaurants, even the buses.

She entered the café almost by accident. One minute she was standing outside watching as people tucked into bacon and eggs and pots of tea, the next minute she was seated inside with a round of toast on the way. She looked around, at the unfamiliar surroundings, at the unfamiliar faces, and wondered what she, a fourteen-year-old girl on the run, should do now. As she pondered this thought, a young man turned round the chair opposite her and down, his chin resting on the back of the chair. He was in his late teens with beautiful blue eyes and a cheeky smile. He wore expensive clothes.

"Have you got a spare cigarette?"

"No, sorry."

He reached across the table and produced two Lambert and Butlers from behind her ear.

"Liar!"

He handed one of them to her and smiled his cheeky smile. She blushed.

"I'm Jake. You just arrived?" he asked, gesturing

to the bag by her feet.

"Yeah."

"Have you got anywhere to stay?"

"No, not yet."

"Well don't worry, I know a place, it's real cheap. Clean too. But first I'm gonna show you around. I'm an excellent guide."

She smiled bashfully.

After some tea and toast, Jake took her on the underground. It was so busy, four queues of weird and wonderful people snaking down escalators that went on for miles. Jake jumped up on the metal barrier separating two of the escalators, grabbed her hand and pulled her up.

"What are you doing?" she asked, teetering to one side as commuters cast them both dirty looks.

"Trust me."

He began to run down the barrier. Miss Richards followed. Terrified at first, by the time they reached the end and had vaulted the automatic barriers she felt exhilarated. They made it onto a train just as the doors were closing, a flustered guard trailing in their wake.

They got off at Charing Cross, once again vaulting the barriers and running up the steps to the echo of angry voices. Jake grabbed a Mars Bar from a vendor on the way past and threw it to her.

"You're mental!" she shouted.

"You better believe it!" and they burst out into the daylight.

They made the short walk to Westminster arm-in-arm.

"It's huge!" she exclaimed. "So much bigger than

it looks on the sauce bottles."

"Full of crooks that is. Biggest den of thieves in England!"

They bought chips and ate them walking along the South Bank. Home, her father, all of that misery, couldn't have been further from her thoughts. Jake was so funny and so kind. And so exciting.

He was as good as his word too. He found Miss Richards a place to stay and helped get her settled. He also got her a job. Working as one of his girls.

And so it began. She had escaped one of hell's many rooms only to be locked in another. Her life moved from Gin Lane to The Harlot's Progress. In the months and years that followed she passed from one pimp and lowlife to another, gathering habits and scars along the way.

When she was sixteen, she read a newspaper article about teenage runaways, which included a photograph of herself. It was an old picture. Taken when she was much younger. It could have been anybody. The article stated that she had last been seen boarding a bus to London. Her and countless others.

Years later, she encountered Stephen. He was a nice enough guy. Too stupid to be anything else. Too trusting. His story was predictable enough. Marriage on the rocks. Kids out of control. One day he turned up at Miss Richards' place of employment and promptly fell in love with her. Why was something she could never fathom. Just because she happened to be there was the only reason she could think of. But love her he did. To the point of blindness.

"Do you have it?" she had asked nervously. She was like a cat on the hunt, her eyes wide and alert.

"Here it is," and he slipped her a small package.

It was exactly what he said it was. Couldn't be anything else. And yet she looked at it over and over again, expecting the mirage to eventually disappear.

"You sure?"

"Yes, yes, I'm positive. It's guaranteed to work – and then we can be together." He kissed her.

"Oh baby," she whispered. "You know I can't wait."

"Everything is arranged. I've written the letter to Kate. By the time she reads it we'll be long gone."

"You know where to meet?"

"Yes, at the Northampton services. In the car park. I don't see why we can't meet nearer…"

"Because it's not safe! Listen to me, look at me."

He did.

"This is deadly serious. If I ever thought anything might happen to you because of me I wouldn't be able live with myself. You've done enough for me…for us."

"I'll do anything you want. You only have to ask."

"You've done more than you should."

As Stephen left, he pressed a handful of notes into her hand.

The stuff worked exactly as it was supposed to. Baz, her latest owner, went out like a light. She stood over him for a while, watching his sleeping form, her breathing as low as she could for fear he might wake and kill her. It was a feeling she remembered as much as experienced. Like reliving a bad dream. He was unconscious. One hundred percent. He wouldn't wake up for hours. She knew this. It was fact. And yet she refused to believe it. For half an hour or more she just stood there. Watching.

Then a thought flashed across her mind. The time, only last week, he'd made her do a group of guys. City types. Drunk. Violent. She thought of the things they did to her. Of the man grinning behind the camera. And Baz's shrug of the shoulders when she told him.

She grabbed everything of value. The drugs. The money. The knocked-off jewellery. All of it.

The petrol can seemed smaller now that she was pouring its contents over the room. At first she poured it around and away from Baz, fearing the smell might wake him up. But soon the viscous liquid was dribbling over his face and body. He didn't stir.

Miss Richards felt remarkably calm yet her hands trembled as she picked up the lighter off the coffee table. She held it out as far as she could, her whole body leaning forward as though it were a tree hanging precariously over the side of the cliff, the furthest extended branch hanging uneasily. Tentatively.

This was it. Now or never. Don't and Baz would haunt her forever. Do it and Baz would be erased. There would be no comeback. But a whole host of new problems would stalk her. She'd be a murderer. They would hunt her. They would hunt her and find her and she'd spend the rest of her life in prison. In another prison.

The thoughts spun round and round inside her head. She talked herself into doing it, then out of doing it, then into doing it again, until the arguments became so entangled and were travelling so fast that she could make no sense of them.

Then Baz did stir. His nose twitched. Just a little. The lighter fell to the floor and Miss Richards fled. She never saw him again. She never saw Stephen either.

She knew that Baz would try to find her, to kill her or, worse still, deliver her full circle to the life she'd fled. That fear guided her but it did not plague her. Miss Richards had been running and hiding for most of her existence. It was the only life she knew. Fear was her bedfellow and together they treaded carefully by day and slept lightly at night.

She chose Edinburgh because to her Scotland seemed a million miles from London. Only it wasn't. London was still extremely close. The money she pilfered rapidly disappeared. Old habits die hard and the ones still breathing were the costliest. She worked the game to keep her nose powdered even though she'd fled to escape that very life.

She would stop, of course, once she had enough cash to get off the island and start again somewhere else. Hers was just a temporary situation. It had ever been thus.

Now twenty four, her life was finally beginning to turn around. Yes, she was still on the game. Yes, she still did drugs, but only coke, weed and the occasional upper. But she was no longer a kept animal. A pet forced to perform tricks on cue by twisted psychopaths. Now she was her own woman, free to work where she wanted, when she wanted. No one barking orders or extracting cash by force. No more rapes or beatings at the hands of supposed lovers. Such an improvement was impossible to measure.

She had dreams of a better life. Of a different world. There was a vague image in her mind, one taken from magazines and television. She saw a house, simple and made of white wood. It sat on a ridge overlooking a beautiful, sun-kissed beach. She imagined sitting on the veranda, basking in the warm glow of the sun, watching the waves lapping the shore.

Someone was there too. She had never pictured their face, hadn't dared to, but they were always there. She wasn't even sure if that person was a man or a woman. It didn't matter. That person was warm and kind, and the two of them were very much in love. She imagined their warm touch, drawing breath at the thought of their hand brushing her arm, of their lips softly caressing her neck. The beauty of these things could never be fully captured in her mind, no matter how hard she concentrated. There was a feeling within her that would well up and, as her skin tingled, she could feel herself tantalisingly close to knowing that feeling. Of knowing pure love. But she didn't. She knew only delusion and desperate longing. The beach was far, far away.

Having gathered up the offending sheets, Miss Richards shuffled through to the main room, carrying the bundle under her arm. Part of her wished for another client and more cash, the other hoped for a rest and a long, self-indulgent shower.

There were no customers to speak of and so she locked herself in the bathroom. She removed her dress in front of the mirror, the bright light revealing on her arms the tell-tale signs of a now beaten heroin addiction. The lines and wrinkles on her face belied her young age as with so many women on the receiving end of life's kicks and men's fists. Makeup could only paper over the cracks now ingrained.

Stepping into the shower, her body creaked. She was tired and the relaxing cascade of warm water made her more so. Lathering herself with soap, her limbs and muscles ached from the rigours of another exhausting day. And there were still several hours to go.

She stayed under the hot spring for a long while, rubbing her arms, legs and torso as steam clung in equatorial clouds around her ears. Aquatic droplets sprinkled the tiles: dripping, falling, reforming. She imagined herself bathing in a hot spring at the foot of a great mountain, the chirp of exotic birds and the scent of wild flowers all around her. Then a voice drifted across the lush tropical mist from the unwelcome cold outside.

"Cindy? Remember you've got a five o'clock!"

"Is he here yet?"

"No, but he will be any minute!"

Miss Richards blew a raspberry at the frosted glass door, turned off the shower and stepped through the haze. She quickly dried herself then wiped away the film of liquid that covered the surface next to the washbasin. Reaching into her handbag, she produced a small tin and a crisp twenty-pound note. The freshest she had. The tin bore an incomprehensibly intricate pattern. Black and white squiggles entangled into impossible shapes. Inside, though, was pure white.

Thick crystallised powder gleamed up at her; shining and sparkling like a thousand tiny diamonds. Using the reverse side of a nail file, Miss Richards scooped up a generous measure of the white dynamite and heaped it onto the Formica. She retrieved a bankcard from her wallet and skilfully chopped herself a fat line, shuffling the powder back and forth several times with the plastic.

When she was completely satisfied with her work she rolled up the note between her thumb and forefinger, placed one end inside her left nostril, covered the right one, and snorted hard. Bit by bit the diamonds disappeared. On finishing, she tilted her head back slightly and sniffed long and hard, rubbing her nose and a fair proportion of her face with the back of her hand.

Bullseye!

She winced momentarily as the bitter chemicals reacted on her taste buds. Then it was gone and she perked-up. Full of beans. Raring to go. It was her first line since lunch and really hit the spot. Cleansed, refreshed and feeling rather nice, she returned to business.

Her five o'clock arrived bang on time. A balding, frail old man in his sixties. He was into being dominated, which was a bonus as she could whip and beat him to her heart's content as he lay face down and helpless, trussed up like a mental patient. He did insist on sex too, which was unpleasant if predictably short.

"Is that okay?" she asked. "It's not too tight, is it?"

His head shook and instantly Miss Richards turned into a witch, howling and cackling as she tortured his decrepit frame with leather and birch.

"You dirty bastard, you've been a bad boy! Mistress Cindy is going to have to punish you!"

"I'm…I'm…sorry Mistress Cindy…I won't do it again…I promise," he whimpered.

"Fuckin' right you won't!"

The whole show was over in twenty minutes, bondage and all. He left a ton lighter.

The next gentleman to arrive was one of Natalie's regulars. He always came on Friday evenings. While Natalie and he got down to whatever sordid business he sought, Miss Richards sat idly in front of the television, chain smoking and yapping to her boss about fashion and the weather.

The phone rang incessantly. Each time her boss would fire off information – names, times, places, prices. She became furious with one caller, telling him that she would phone the police before slamming down the receiver.

"You wouldn't believe that one, Cindy!" she exasperated. "Sick fucker was only asking for kids!"

"Bastard!" replied Miss Richards with little animation.

Just as Natalie's client was leaving, a booking was made. Due in ten minutes, he was reliably described as "young and terrified".

"Hope he's no a fuckin' virgin!" replied Natalie, "I cannae be fucked wi' them."

Natalie had all the class of a package holiday in

Magaluf and the subtlety of an articulated lorry. The woman carried a shrill whine of a voice, which she wielded like a sword and could cut through a person with the sharp efficiency of cheese-wire. Miss Richards especially hated when she asked "what?" which was all too often. It sounded like "waaaaaah?" and agitated the eardrum considerably, even from the other side of the room.

"You iver dun a virgin afore, Cindy?" she continued.

"Yeah, a few times."

"Half the fuckin' time yer feart they'll pish themselves!"

"I think it's kinda sweet," countered Miss Richards.

"Pathetic if you ask me," piped up their boss. "Some of them young enough to be my grandson!"

Natalie sniggered. Miss Richards did not. The coke was wearing off. As it always did. Charlie, like the brazen thief that he was, didn't hang around for long. Having emptied her wallet, he would throw Miss Richards a contemptuous, mocking leer and hurriedly depart, his arrogant laugh ringing haughtily in her ears. Then he was gone. And even though she knew him to be a scoundrel and a liar, she still wanted him back. Immediately.

She had to be strong, however. She had to resist his charms and persuasion.

Another line would be great though…wouldn't it?

He encouraged her as he always did.

"Come on, darling, you know how good we are together."

Whispering softly. Tenderly. Invitingly.

"It'll be different this time, I promise."

Only it never was.

"I've changed."

Only he never did.

She still wanted another line. She really wanted another line. Just the one. She'd been telling herself all day that she should keep what dwindling amount she had left for the evening. She'd have a long soak in the tub, a nice meal washed down with a bottle of wine and then snort a huge line and smoke skunk in front of the TV until she passed out. That was the plan and she intended to stick to it. 'Just the one' would lead to another, and another, and another.

And yet she really needed some more. Just a little. Charlie kept whispering sweet nothings. She still had a couple of hours to go. More grime and muck to wade through. More scumbags. A wee whiff of coke and she'd breeze it. Just a cheeky one to see her home. It wouldn't make any difference…would it?

The amount of coke she had, the amount she needed, and how to get it, whizzed around inside her brain at a million miles an hour. It always did. She didn't have enough for the weekend. That was for sure. She had ample for that evening but would probably wake up on Saturday with none and be strung out all afternoon. Meeting Charlie could be difficult during the day. He was always sleeping or elsewhere. On a Friday night, though, Charlie was really easy to find. Too easy.

It wasn't as though she couldn't afford to buy any anyway…was it? It would definitely make more sense to get some straight after work and, therefore, having another line now wouldn't make any difference...would it?

But what if she couldn't get any? What if Charlie had gone AWOL? A bird in the hand and all that. Besides, surely it was time she started easing off her habit? It was the white stuff that kept her yoked to this lifestyle. It was an addiction she could well do without. It would be best to wait until she got home, take all her coke in one go and then never take any ever again...wouldn't it? But a line would be great right now. Just the one mind. Just a wee one...

As Miss Richards debated the implications of such actions, the buzzer rang and the next appointment arrived. Back to business. She'd worry about Charlie later.

The receptionist returned with a lad still in his teens.

"Girls this is...sorry, what did you say your name was again?"

"Michael."

"Michael, Michael. Yes, of course, Michael." As she spoke she gestured to him with exaggerated hand movements and a sickly grin.

"Right Michael. These are our two girls. This is Natalie, and this is Cindy."

Both women smiled sympathetically.

"Now, which girl would you like for your massage? Remember there's no rush."

The boy studied both girls nervously, his eyes flitting between the pair awkwardly, trying to gauge their attractiveness without staring at either of them for very long. Eventually and inevitably he settled for Miss Richards.

"I'd like to go with you," he murmured, pointing at her feebly. "If that's okay?"

"Sure," smiled Miss Richards. Easy money.

"Okay then, Michael," said the receptionist, ushering him to his feet. "If you'd just like to come this way, Cindy will look after you."

Miss Richards assisted him to the bedroom as though he were an invalid. He sat trembling on the edge of the bed, anxiously glancing around, not knowing where to look or what to say. An unnerving silence filled the room.

"Why don't you take your clothes off?" she asked soothingly.

He followed her suggestion, leaving on his boxer shorts through which a hardening and surprisingly large penis was visible.

"Listen, there's nothing to worry about. Just relax."

As she approached him he gulped. She embraced him, wrapping her arms around his shivering form and running her fingers through his short hair as her breasts pressed against him.

"Okay?"

"Mmmm…"

"Right," she whispered in his ear. "It's ten pound for the massage. Shall I take that now?"

Miss Richards wanted to make sure she at least got this in case he ran away.

He fumbled around in his trouser pockets, eventually finding a sports wallet. Shyly, he handed her a dog-eared ten-pound note. Noticing it hadn't been alone, she accepted it with a smile and asked him to lie on his front on the bed. This he did, having to wriggle himself into a comfortable position over his now raging hard-on. She knelt over him and began tenderly rubbing baby oil into his pimply white skin.

"Is that nice?"

"Mmmm…mmmm…yeah…"

"Good."

She massaged him slowly, first kneading his back and skinny arms, then his legs, moving all the way down to his feet, which she tickled and caressed. With one quick pull she removed his shorts before moving closer so that she was practically lying on top of him. As she blew softly in his ear and kissed the back of his neck, she pressed her breasts firmly against his oily spine. Pulling up her dress, she rubbed her hot, naked crotch against his bottom. Delicately, she licked his earlobes as one hand slipped between his buttocks, touching first between his cheeks, then lower onto his testicles, then out again. She repeated this motion several times as her other hand massaged his inner thigh, each time staying that little bit longer between his legs. Eventually she reached under his body and began stroking the entire length of his penis as he groaned with surprised pleasure. She reckoned it to be eight, maybe nine inches long and with considerable girth too. So out of place compared to the rest of his puny physique.

"Is there anything else I can do for you?" she asked, pulling on him.

"Mmmm…em…like what?"

"Like me sucking your cock?"

"Mmmm…yes…I'd like that…"

"How about fucking me?"

She emphasised and prolonged the F word. He flinched.

"Em…I'd like that too."

"I'm afraid it'll cost you a bit extra."

"Em…how much?"

Looking at him intently in the mirror, she rattled off the prices for oral and for sex, subtracting the ten pounds he had already paid her. His face dropped.

"What's the matter? Don't you have enough?"

"I really want sex…but I'm a fiver short."

"Give me what you've got and I'll let you fuck me," she announced, winking at him.

Handing her an assortment of crumpled notes and copper shrapnel, he looked like Christmas had come early.

"So, Michael, have you ever done it before?"

"Yes…yes, I have."

His nose grew that little bit longer.

"Right, well lie back and relax. You'll have never had it this good before, I promise you!"

He did as he was instructed, gazing at her in wonder. Slowly, sensuously, she peeled off her tight dress, her eyes transfixed on his. As she revealed her nipples she smiled, winked, and then licked her lips seductively. She cupped her breasts and pulled on them, stretching them as far as they could go as the straps of her dress dangled tantalisingly. Slowly, she stood up, until she towered over him. She kicked off her stilettos and wiggled her torso above the young man's gaping jaw. As she pulled the dress up around her thighs she flashed him pouts and smiles.

Eventually, to his awe and amazement, her furry vagina was revealed. She let the dress fall to her feet and kicked it away. Opening her legs directly over him, she spread back her lips with nailed fingers. Exaggeratedly, she sucked on her index finger and guided it in and out of herself as she gyrated above him, retaining eye contact throughout. Beside himself with excitement, the young man tugged furiously at his penis.

"Yeah, that's it! Wank over me!"

He winced, indicating he might jump the gun. She couldn't have that. Not until they had briefly copulated. She whipped out a condom, which she quickly pulled down over him using her mouth. He gasped from this new and uncomfortable sensation. She applied some lubricant and straddled him. He lay there amazed and breathless as she slid down onto his bold erection. It took her a few seconds to get it all the way in and she had to stop halfway to reposition herself before sliding down to the hilt. He felt even bigger than he looked and despite her years of experience, it still felt uncomfortable as she moved up and down on him.

The boy was in heaven. Groaning like an animal, his eyeballs somersaulted as his sweaty palms grabbed excitedly at her breasts. He pulled himself up and tried to lick her nipples but was unsuccessful, instead falling back onto the bed where he lay gazing up in wonder at her as she rode him.

She began profaning, turning the air blue with coarse verse in the hope that this would force a reaction. It did, but not the desired one. Rather than tip him over the edge, she merely fanned his flames and he began to shunt. Hard and fast. He was pushing in the opposite direction to her and they soon lost all rhythm. She gestured him to stop, which he ignored. Trying to fight back her annoyance, she climbed off him and commanded him to go on top. This didn't seem to disappoint him and he immediately leapt up, his tongue hanging dementedly out of the side of his mouth. As she lay on her back, Miss Richards had to fend him off until she had lubricated herself enough to accept him. He was insatiable.

"Take it easy," she muttered. "I'll do it."

Slowly she guided him into her once more.

"Come on, Michael… fuck me… come inside me… come inside me, Michael!" she bawled in frustration.

"I want to fuck you doggy," he announced, all virginal shyness now exorcised.

"Okay. But, please, do it gently."

He grabbed hold of her bottom and slid back and forth as hard as before. He would start off slowly but always ended up at the same, painful speed. She had to stop periodically to re-lubricate. Every time he would wait impatiently, then carry on as before, battering her with all that he could muster.

The clock on the wall told Miss Richards that they had been at it for over half an hour.

"Look, your time's nearly up," she remarked, exhausted. "I'll have to finish you by hand."

She pulled off the condom and gripped his length tightly, wrenching his foreskin up and down over his helmet. She did this until her hand went numb and then changed hands.

"Come on…come on!" she bawled. "Hurry up!"

"I'm trying…I'm trying!"

She licked his testicles and sucked on them hard, almost biting at them, giving him oral he hadn't paid for.

"Ooooooh! That's fucking class! Suck it. Ahh…I'm gonna come!"

He grabbed his penis and fired with a yell. Thick jets of come splattered across her face and hair, coating her in a sticky blizzard of white mucous.

"Jesus…"

He left grinning from ear to ear.

In the bathroom she soothed herself with cooling ointment, then filled her nose with the bulk of the cocaine she had intended to save. She would definitely have to buy more.

Back on form, she sat beside Natalie in the lounge and babbled.

"Fuck sake! I tell you, that boy could go, he really could, I couldn't believe it, unbelievable, like a train he just kept going, on and on and on, wouldn't stop…"

Similar to the way she was now talking.

"Get away!" retorted a disbelieving Natalie.

"No, honestly, he just kept going and going, I really…"

"Anymore punters to come?"

"Just the one. He should be here soon."

Turning to Natalie, she replied "You can have him!"

"He wants you both."

"Ah well, no rest for the wicked," and she burst into a fit of giggles, which she stifled as quickly as she could.

Her brain was flying in orbit around the room. Sucking furiously on her cigarette, she tried to remain calm. Glaring at the TV, she was unable to stifle the occasional inane giggle. Time dragged on until, finally, the buzzer signalled the late arrival of their last act of the evening.

Standing just over six feet and well built, the man was strikingly handsome with cropped dark hair and a muscular body. Miss Richards actually went weak at the knees as she stood up to greet him, though that was probably due more to the marching powder.

In the bedroom his manner was cocky. Self-assured. Confident without being vain, he was completely at ease in such company. Natalie dressed in black leather while Miss Richards became 'Nurse Cindy'. All very kinky. By the end all three of them were exhausted. He headed out on the town to get hammered with his mates while the women cleaned up, another day of sleaze over and done with.

Miss Richards made her way to the corner shop on autopilot. Her head was confused by the usual dilemmas. To buy coke or not to buy coke. That was the question.

As she bought a packet of cigarettes from the jovial shopkeeper she brought out her mobile and texted her supplier. Charlie would be coming round tonight. Miss Richards left the shop in such a hurry she forgot to take her change.

Mr Palavar

The shopkeeper chuckled and set the change aside. He was a large man with a stomach that protruded at right-angles from his chest and arched into a bulbous mound that curved back into his trousers as a perfect sphere. His arms seemed terribly short and too thin to support such large hands, which were worn and scarred. The man's skin was incredibly dark, almost black but not quite, there being a rich mahogany quality to it. Only the palms of his hands differed and were a pale pink.

His face was worn, its chequered terrain bearing deep valleys and bumpy hills. Springy tufts of silver hair burst from around his chin, interspersed with patches of snow. The main feature of his face, however, was the irrepressible smile that never left it. His cheery, jovial expression was infectious, likely to cause an epidemic in a crowded place.

Mrs Doherty shuffled in to buy her Evening News. He already had it ready and folded for her as she approached the counter.

"How are you, Edna?"

"Och fine, Mr Palavar, fine. I'm seeing Mary the night."

Mary was one of Mrs Doherty's many, many grandchildren.

"She's expecting, you know?"

"Yes, yes, you mentioned it."

Mrs Doherty had mentioned little else for over two months.

"How many great grandchildren will that make?"

"Four. Wee Bobby, Darren, Kylie and then this one."

"You're some woman!"

"Aye, and you're still the charmer!"

It was not long before Mr Palavar felt peckish. He always felt peckish. His rounded figure was testament to an appetite that was never quite satisfied. He ate constantly while he worked, replacing set meals with incessant nibbling. Whenever there was a quiet moment he would duck through the back for a quick bite. He ate with gusto, savouring every mouthful as though it were his last.

In the back of the shop, beyond the counter, was Mr Palavar's space. It wasn't much, no more than a cupboard really. He often mused that it resembled the cell he'd once occupied. At least in size. Welikada was always with him.

In the corner was a small fridge, which was bare save for a bottle of water and a large plate wrapped in metal foil. There was a slight whiff of sour pickles and yogurt, and the nip of fresh chilli. The foil made a satisfying rustle as he removed it; a wonderfully pungent aroma filled the room.

On the plate were six small metal bowls that formed a circle around a stack of white-ish objects. Each bowl's contents were a different colour: bright green, vibrant red, earthy brown. Each had its own peculiar scent and taste too. Each had a place in Mr Palavar's heart.

The white-ish objects were hoppers – pancakes made from rice and coconut milk. Sweet and at the same time savoury. Spongy yet also crispy. Mr Palavar's staple, the hoppers acted as a canvas onto which he painted his culinary masterpiece. He retrieved a spoon from the sink and washed it. This was to be his paintbrush.

First he scooped some yellow rice onto the uppermost hopper. The rice was fragrant, infused with cardamom and lemongrass and enlivened with saffron. To that he added a small measure of mint sambol, a green sundry both fresh and spicy. He contemplated for a moment his next brushstroke. There was pork badum – spicy and rich. But also king prawns – hot and sweet with the tang of tomatoes. He deliberated a second, then brushed a liberal spoonful of the pork across the hopper. He finished it off with some fresh yogurt to counteract the heat. As always, his hopper was too full and all manner of juices escaped as he awkwardly wrapped it into a parcel. The result was a messy, dripping bundle that would explode in his mouth. He lifted it exultantly to his lips and took a hearty bite.

The exterior of the hopper was crispy and this was the first sensation, followed by the taste of coconut. As he savoured the pancake's taste and texture, the rush of chilli jolted him forward: an intense fire that spread out over his mouth and down his throat. The mint's cool freshness mingled with the heat, delivering his palette into a purgatorial paradise. Pockets of flavour burst on his tongue, carrying aromatic fireballs to his stomach and nostrils.

In a few seconds his masterpiece was no more and he stood with his hands resting on his giant belly, smiling contentedly. Then the urge for a second gripped him. One with prawns and coconut sambol, and slightly less rice. He licked his lips, wiped his hands on an old Royal Wedding tea towel, and spooned a large chunk of tangy date and lime pickle into his mouth to refresh his palette.

The tinkle of a bell, however, forced him through to the front of the shop. Customers arrived in fits and bursts, forming impromptu and short-lived groups, an empty shop becoming a busy one in a matter of seconds. Mr Palavar greeted each with the same kindness and enthusiasm but his mind was fixed firmly on those wee metal dishes.

A brief lull allowed him to nip through the back for his second hopper, which he wolfed down before returning to his station. On the wall, above the magazines, was a dusty old map, its corners brown and curled with age. That, and his wife's sumptuous cooking, were the only reminders of Mr Palavar's past life. So worn was the map that the old island was barely visible, much as it was in his own mind. A fading memory that remained alive but seemed less and less real with each passing day. A tropical paradise Mr Palavar would never see again. Serendib.

Sixteen years had passed since he last felt the air turn heavy, signalling the arrival of the steamy monsoon. Sixteen years since he'd plucked ripe mangoes straight from the tree, tearing at their skin with his fingernails. Sixteen years since he'd stared down the barrel of an assault rifle.

Mr Palavar's family had sold carpets in Colombo for generations. The spirit of the entrepreneur was passed down to Mr Palavar's father and then on to him. His future was mapped out. He would work for the family business, eventually taking charge before, one day, passing it on to his own son. That had been

Mr Palavar's destiny and he was never anything other than grateful and excited by the prospect.

1983 changed all of that.

That year had promised so much. Recently married and with a child on the way, the pieces of his life were falling into place. The business was prospering and new ventures in India presented themselves. But the island was stirring.

Mr Palavar's younger brother, Chenjurin – a quiet, introspective boy compared with his boisterous older brother – had gone to university the year before. There he became radicalised into an advocate of the Tamil struggle. A struggle the rest of the family had little understanding of or time for. He had travelled north to Tamil country and talked with great passion and anger of the poverty and injustice he had witnessed. He talked of retribution, of revolution. He talked of war.

On 23rd July 1983, as the family were clearing up supper, Mr Palavar's father turned on the wireless, as he normally did after a meal. The sombre newscaster reported that Tamil terrorists had attacked an army patrol near Jaffna. It had begun.

Two hours later there was a heavy thud at the door and loud voices demanded to be let in. Mr Palavar answered and was immediately knocked to the ground. Several armed men in khaki surrounded the family.

They were looking for Chen but in his absence Mr Palavar was dragged out into the street. A crowd had already gathered, local people some of whom Mr Palavar recognised. They spat and snarled, some aiming kicks at his body as he was thrown into the back of a truck.

The truck drove to a military base some way outside the city. Interrogation began at once and lasted for hours. The same questions repeated over and over, punctuated by varying threats and acts of violence. Every time he gave the same answer and it was clear that he knew nothing. And yet the interrogations continued.

After two days of torture and hunger, he and a dozen other captives were thrown in a truck. A short while later they reached Welikada Prison. A place of no return.

Today Mr Palavar had all but shut that dark period from his mind. Memories only returned as brief and mercifully rare flashbacks. Sometimes he would be jolted by electrodes as he stacked shelves, other times he would move uncomfortably in bed as objects were inserted into him. But one memory, one night, shone through the darkness and could never be erased.

He was lying in his cell, hungry, tired and half-conscious from another beating. There was a roaring in his ears, brought on from the physical abuse and at first he believed the strange and worrying sounds beyond the cell walls were a manifestation of that. Even when he heard screaming and shouting he still believed this to be imagined and did not stir from his foetal position. It was only when the smell of burning became unmistakeable that he knew this was no dream.

He feared that the prison was on fire and that, locked away and forgotten, he would be left to perish in the inferno. He hauled himself over to the door and thumped on it, crying for help as best he could. No one came.

After a while the smell of burning vanished. The screams continued into the night, however, and every sound seemed magnified and of great significance as he waited and prayed.

The turning of a key in the lock brought with it the same mixture of emotions: fear of being beaten and killed; hope that much needed food and water was on its way; and a deeper, irrational hope that this was all a dream. And there was the added feeling of curiosity.

The guard kicked him hard in the stomach, told him that several Tamil dogs had been cleansed and that he would be next. He was then blindfolded and dragged through the prison. He received several blows along the way and passed out. When he came to he was in a large cell with about a dozen fellow prisoners, their faces were haunted and pale, as they recounted the previous night's rioting by Sinhalese prisoners.

"It was all setup," whispered a bedraggled old man with only one eye. "They deliberately let them out to kill us."

Two days later, completely unexpectedly, Mr Palavar was released. No explanation was given, no apology was offered. He was simply taken to the gates and told "you can go." He wanted to fall to his knees and lovingly kiss the earth beneath his feet but, fearing it might be a horrible trick, he fled, running until he collapsed from exhaustion.

He woke in a crowded hospital ward, his filthy bed shared with a legless child who died a short while later. Mr Palavar remained confined to that bed for two days, barely able to stand, desperately waiting for news. None came. The hospital was stretched to bursting. Chaos reigned. His was just one of countless tragedies being played out across the island.

On the third day a visitor did arrive, a man Mr Palavar recognised but did not know. He had lived in the same street and worked for the city administration. They had exchanged no more than a few words in all the time they had been neighbours. The man looked ragged and frightened, like a hunted animal. He spoke in whispers, forever turning his head and eyes around the ward, particularly in the direction of the door.

"Your family…they are safe."

"Where are they?"

"In a camp outside the city."

"How do you know this?" his eyes widened.

"I just do."

"Can you show me where it is?" Mr Palavar was so overcome with excitement his knees trembled violently, causing the bed to shake.

"They're at Ratmalana airport," he hissed. "The government has a camp there. All the Tamils from Colombo are leaving. The city isn't safe anymore."

As the man got up to leave, Mr Palavar grabbed his arm.

"What happened to you? And why are you helping me?"

"They killed my wife."

"But you're Sinhalese!"

"We are suffering too."

The man left hastily, a noticeable limp in his gait.

As soon as he was able, Mr Palavar left the hospital and followed the man's directions. The visit had filled him with hope but he also had to prepare for disappointment or else it would crush him. And so his mind flitted between two extremes – of being reunited with his family, and of never seeing them again – as he dragged his battered frame in the direction of Ratmalana Airport.

The camp was a sea of misery. Mr Palavar crawled to a medical tent where his wounds were tended to by a French doctor. Able to walk again, albeit with a limp, he joined a mass of people, thousands of them, crowded round a series of wooden tables. He waited there for several hours, exhausted by the heat, exchanging tales of woe with his new neighbours.

"I'm looking for my wife. I was... we became separated two weeks ago. I was told she was here." and he looked about him, taking in the enormity of the place. "Somewhere..."

"If she is here you will find her, I am sure of that."

Others weren't so sure.

"There's no organisation. The services are completely overwhelmed. They didn't plan for this even though they caused it," and she fired a vicious stare at a nearby soldier. "I haven't seen my brothers since the riots. I have no idea where they are, if they're alive at all. This isn't like '58. Mark my words, they won't stop until they've driven us all into the Gulf of Mannar!"

There was also talk of retribution.

"They've made war with us. There's no turning back. As soon as I get out of here I'll join the Tigers and kill as many of those bastards as I possibly can!"

Mr Palavar didn't know what to think. Thoughts of war and revenge were far from his mind. All he sought was to be reunited, to see his beloved wife again, to touch her soft skin and gaze into those wonderful eyes once more.

He asked every person he came into contact with the same question. "Do you know her? Have you seen her?" And every time he was given a weary shake of the head in return.

As night fell, Mr Palavar reached the end of the queue and was processed. He was shown to a mattress and given a blanket and some rations. And again he was told his wife's whereabouts where not known. He was now officially an IDP – Internally Displaced Person. He had entered the ranks of the dispossessed.

The next morning, Mr Palavar began searching the camp for his family, asking every person he passed the same question over and over. He did this all morning until blisters forced him to rest. He had no shoes and the skin around his heels had rubbed away to reveal deep red scars. As he was examining them, he heard a familiar voice in the distance.

"I need to make sure I get enough for everyone."

The voice tailed off and when Mr Palavar looked up its owner was not in view. He leapt up and stood on his tiptoes, despite the pain, trying to get a view over the crowd. That's when he saw him making his way purposefully through the throng. A man he never thought he'd be pleased to see.

Robert Perundhevan McIntyre was of an old Christian family and had always planned for his eldest daughter to marry a Christian. His wife, however, was a forceful character and good friends with the Palavars. She was content for her daughter to marry any man so long as he was upstanding, kind and had the means to support her. From the day the wedding was planned, Robert treated his prospective son-in-law with an embittered and cold indifference, his pleasant manner during the traditional Hindu ceremony forced and short-lived. He and Mr Palavar barely communicated beyond formal pleasantries, Robert's under duress.

At this moment, however, the sight of his father-in-law, the ubiquitous seriousness of his posture, brought about in Mr Palavar a sort of euphoria. Forgetting the blisters, he charged through the crowd and jumped on him, nearly knocking him to the ground.

"My God – you're alive!"

Robert maintained the stony expression he was born with but there was a tenderness in his eyes and he couldn't help reciprocating the embrace.

"Anadi's okay. She's nearby – I will take you to her."

Mr Palavar promptly fainted.

What followed was dreamlike. He found himself surrounded by relatives and family friends who fussed over him, bringing him food and water, and an American doctor who treated his wounds and fever. His parents were there and his wife, and there was also a tiny newborn baby called Murugan whom he was told was his son.

"He came early."

For the most part Mr Palavar was catatonic and smiled vacantly, his body in a stupor, his mind confused and incurably tired. Several days passed.

Eventually his mind returned to health and the tiredness lifted. He interacted with his loved ones and held little Muri for the first time. He learned too of their journey to the camp. When the mobs started looting and burning, a kindly Sinhalese couple provided sanctuary to many Tamil families, housing them in their basement until it was safe to travel out of the city. Mr Palavar's visitor in the hospital now made sense.

Many of the inhabitants were moving to camps in the north and the family decided to follow. They were soon crowded on a boat headed for Jaffna. The north was Tamil country yet none of them had ever been there before. The only one who had was Chen and there was still no word on him. The north was supposed to provide sanctuary but in reality it was as dangerous as the south. Here the Tamil insurgents were in open conflict with the military and by night shells could be heard exploding worryingly close to the camp. There was still no respite from war.

When the chance came to move again, across the water to Tamil Nadu in southern India, the family grasped it. India was a safe haven. Whatever lay in store for them there, the fighting would not follow.

They set sail once more, their status changing from that of internally displaced people to fully-fledged refugees. They were now at the mercy of the international system. Not only homeless but stateless. Welcomed by India but at the same time not welcome.

The camp in Tamil Nadu was much the same as that in Jaffna – row upon row of tents for as far as the eye could see; fences to keep the captives in; armed soldiers to keep order; the same helpless inertia and boredom.

When hope arrived it was from a most unexpected source. A letter arrived postmarked 'London, UK' and addressed to Mr Palavar. It looked innocuous enough: a plain white envelope, small, thin and light. The handwriting was that of a man, somewhat crooked and bunched up at one end where the writer had ran out of space.

Inside was a single piece of paper with just a few words scrawled in English:

> I understand that you and the rest of the family are safe. This is a great relief for us. I also hear that you now have a child. I would like to extend an invitation for you, your wife and son to visit us in London. There you can start a new life.
>
> You will soon be visited by a delegate from the British Embassy who will arrange your passage to England.
>
> Yours sincerely,
> (Uncle) Rajesekaran Kalaparan

Uncle Raj had been a rogue and a gambler. In 1950s Colombo his drinking, gambling and womanising exploits were legendary.

In a desperate attempt to rein him in, the family arranged his marriage to a decent young lady. Raj had other plans, however, and created a storm when he eloped to London with a famous English actress he had wooed in the bar of the Mount Lavinia Hotel the night before his wedding. The family never heard from him again and his name barely received a mention in the years that followed.

Two days later, just as the letter had predicted, a man arrived from the British Embassy. He was earnest looking with serious spectacles and an even more serious suit. He explained to Mr Palavar that the United Kingdom offered a refuge and the opportunity to start a new life. They could be on a plane within a fortnight.

The flight was long and arduous, made worse shortly after take-off when Mr Palavar discovered that he was afraid of flying. He spent the flight with his eyes closed, clasping his wife's hand as tightly as she would allow, breathing deeply and slowly. Little Muri slept throughout.

They were met at Heathrow by a small, unassuming man with dark skin and no hair. His wife was taller than her husband, which wasn't difficult, with white hair that had a purple sheen. Her face was kind but rough and worn with worry lines. Certainly not the bon vivant and glamorous actress Mr Palavar had expected.

"Welcome, welcome!" cried Raj, throwing his arms around them in an exaggerated embrace. "This is Mary - my third wife. The best of the lot!"

Raj's house confirmed that his champagne lifestyle was long gone. He owned a tired old café in Lewisham above which his wife and he lived in a ramshackle flat filled with all kinds of junk ranging from old hat stands to a stuffed brown bear that guarded the hallway with a permanent growl.

Raj and Mary ran the café between them but it was in reality no more than a front for the real business, which was conducted in a basement that could only be accessed via an alleyway.

In contrast to the rest of the house, the basement, which from the outside appeared vacant, was ornately decorated and pristinely clean. The walls were a deep red and patterned with gold. Antique Chinese lanterns hung over several green baize tables that filled most of the room. Here local characters indulged in high-stakes poker. Raj's old habits remained alive and well.

While Mrs Palavar tended to their son, her husband worked in the café and assisted with various things such as stocktaking and dealing with deliveries. This pleased Raj immensely as it allowed him to spend more time in the basement. This benefited all in the household as Raj was a master card sharp and regularly took money or favours from the other gamblers. Although it was never discussed, Mr Palavar was certain that their fast-track migration to the island was thanks to Raj's poker abilities. For although situated in a grotty basement in the East End, Raj's enterprise attracted well-dressed, respectable gentlemen; men of means who would park their fine cars in an abandoned warehouse nearby. Some of the clientele were less salubrious and their presence ensured that no one in the area interfered with either the enterprise or those who frequented it.

After several months Raj invited Mr Palavar into his office for 'a very important chat'. He sat in front of a pile of money, a whisky in one hand and a smile across his face as Mr Palavar nervously took the chair opposite him.

"Don't worry, don't worry, I only have good news for you my boy! I have been working on a few things since…well…since before you arrived. Workwise you understand. I just didn't want to mention anything before everything was arranged, in case it didn't work out."

"And what is this news?" asked Mr Palavar excitedly.

"You know Mustapha?"

Mustapha was a businessman who always wore a tailored suit and never ceased to smile and laugh, regardless of how much money he surrendered at the table. He owned a number of business interests, some of them more legitimate than others.

"Am I to work for him?"

"Of course not! Do you think I would have you working for that crook? No, no, this is all transparent and above board, I promise you."

"Then how does it concern Mustapha?"

"Ha! Mustapha has an old acquaintance, a distant relative in fact. Through marriage. A shopkeeper, originally from Lahore I believe. Well into his eighties and with three sons who have no interest in his family business. He wants to return home before…well…you know…and he wants someone to take over his business."

Mr Palavar's eyes widened.

"It's a grocery shop, no more than that. A bit rundown, needs a lot of work. And these places are like a second wife, you know, they require so much time and attention. Anyway, I have been able to secure this establishment for you at a very reasonable rate, very reasonable indeed. There is, however, a minor complication."

"And what is that?"

"The shop is in Scotland."

Scotland meant very little to Mr Palavar. He only knew that whisky came from there and that it was mountainous. He presumed it to be somewhere else entirely, perhaps continental Europe, or on a separate island somewhere in the Atlantic.

"But how will we get there, and will the Scottish government allow us to stay there?" he asked, bewildered.

Raj laughed so hard his spectacles fell off.

"Scotland is part of the United Kingdom! It's just a few hours north of here."

Two weeks later the Palavars boarded a train at King's Cross and never looked back.

With the shop empty and his belly full, Mr Palavar busied himself by dusting, cleaning and re-arranging his stock. He did this with no set plan in mind; he just wandered around with a cloth and a water sprayer, responding to whatever his eye detected. As he was re-ordering some stock cubes the phone rang.

"How are you, son?" came a familiar voice.

"Things are good, father. I'm going to book the flights tomorrow, really looking forward to it."

"That's great, we can't wait! You're mother's so excited, as always, you know what she gets like!"

Although it took a little longer, Mr Palavar's entire extended family left the refugee camps and started new lives. Most of them, including his parents, moved to Ontario in Canada and every year the family got together to celebrate Diwali. This year it was the Scottish Palavars turn to take the long flight to Toronto.

"Make sure you have enough batteries!"

Mr Palavar found that listening to Mozart eased his fear of flying.

They never did discover what happened to Chen. There were rumours that he lived in the east and had a family. And they had also heard that he had fled to India where he raised funds for the insurgents. Other stories told of a soldier's death shortly after the war began. But it was all conjecture, the truth lost in the fog of war.

His wife had made one hopper larger than the other and Mr Palavar had been saving it for the evening. For his second wind. He filled it with a bit of everything and the sack felt weighty as he brought it to his lips. Several chomps later it was no more. As Mr Palavar wiped the sauce from his chin, another customer entered the shop.

Taylor

A young lad of about twenty, he wore baggy trousers, skater's shoes and a Robocop T-shirt. After a cursory glance at Mr Palavar's wares, he ordered cigarettes, king-size Rizla and an energy drink.

"How are you today young Taylor?" asked Mr Palavar.

"Superb mate, superb!"

"Good, well you behave yourself tonight. Remember your studies come first."

"Yes sir!" and Taylor saluted him jokingly.

Thing was, studies never came first for Taylor. And certainly not on a Friday night. Two hours later he was in a dingy, raucous nightclub and very much in the zone.

The combination of acid, MDMA and speed worked together perfectly. They gripped him in their vice, turning his head and stomach inside out, causing him to fidget, gasp and sigh, to sit down, then stand up, and then sit down again. He wandered around the club in a daze, unsure of what to do or how to do it, his body wriggling through a period of nauseating metamorphosis as his metabolism adjusted to cope with the drugs' immense power.

And…

Then…

BANG!!!

He was there, in that indescribable zone of madness. He felt happy and excited, interested and enthralled, amazed and illuminated. The lights dazzled him, trailing off in various directions around the periphery of his vision. The atmosphere, which was already tremendous so early on in the evening, had him whooping and shouting with unrestrained joy. As he danced, he ran his fingers through his hair, furiously rubbing his scalp, releasing sensations across his face and torso. His jaw swung mechanically.

Taylor floated his way around the club, soaring higher and higher with each beat of the electric snare. The tunes were wicked – hard bass riddled with trippy samples. Each one took the crowd on a journey. Up and up they climbed, the height making them giddy as their arms stretched to the ceiling. Layer upon layer of bass increased the volume and the tempo. As the beats reached their cataclysmic crescendo, everything stopped. For a brief second the whole club hovered, suspended in time, waiting for the next level to kick in. Together they stared over the precipice into the infinity below, ready to leap like lemmings and be caught with an almighty whoosh by a musical magic carpet that would whisk them off up into the stratosphere as the beats returned with a vengeance.

Everyone went mental, surfing on the crest of an enormous soundwave, shouting, cheering, smiling. The entire club was in that magical place, detached from the mundane banality of human existence, transported to the other side. Wild. Untamed. It was like one big happy family, everybody hugging, kissing, pumping palms.

Following a marathon stint on the dance floor Taylor slumped in a plastic chair and relaxed his tired limbs. Closing his eyes, the chaos of the club disappeared as he entered a world of peace and tranquillity. In this inner sanctum all was calm and still. He hunched and then relaxed his shoulders, each tense producing a powerful pulse around his neck and back that contorted his face into expressions of agonised enjoyment. Beneath his resting eyelids there was no light, just a general fuzziness that flickered like an untuned television. The roar of the club dimmed to a hollow, distant echo. He was miles away now, in a state of suspended animation. It was as though his entire body was floating up and away, the rope of reality that tethered him to earth now frayed and ready to snap. Everyone around him was in the same boat, drifting out to sea.

Drawn by the beats, Taylor hauled himself to his feet and delivered himself back into the fray. He hugged and embraced all he knew, inviting them to join him as he made his way to the front where he clambered onto the stage.

He turned to face the throng below, a teeming mass of bodies moulded together into one giant hub of flesh and hair. Arms jutted out in all directions, their hands twisting and turning in the dense air of the club. Incandescent faces shone in the glare of the strobes, each flicker of light revealing a freeze-frame grin or dazed expression.

"Come oooon!"

"Wuh-huh!"

He drew energy from the crowd as though it were a human kinetic battery. The more they danced the more he did, wildly bawling encouragement and beckoning them on. A sea of faces smiled back at him as he sailed above them, conducting their every move from his crow's nest.

In the crowd he spied JP, near the front, his face contorted beyond all recognition as the bass flowed through him. He saw Taylor and waved enthusiastically, then bounded towards the stage with the energy of a small child. He nipped up and onto it in one slick, albeit lucky, movement.

"Taylor! How's it going?" and a bear hug was duly administered.

"Fucking amazing!"

"This is class!" enthused JP, his naked torso glistening with beads of perspiration.

"Are you coming to ours after?"

JP's flat was a den of sin. Taylor almost certainly would.

Burning up in the intense heat, the two of them poured cold water down each other's back, causing them to convulse as the sensation overcame them. Not wanting to miss out, a girl approached them. Taylor coated her shoulders.

"Uhhhh!"

The girl was slim with short fair hair and eyes that were probably blue. It was hard to tell as her irises were overshadowed by gaping black pupils. She certainly looked inviting – soft and cuddly – as most women did to Taylor when he was mashed. Just being near her made him crave a hug or cuddle.

Any sort of bodily contact.

He followed up another pour with a strong if brief massage of her shoulders and then pulled on her hair, rubbing his fingers purposefully over her scalp. She purred with sensual pleasure. Seizing the opportunity, Taylor got close, wrapping his arms around her waist. She told him her name, which he instantly forgot. They kissed, their tongues randomly rubbing against each other.

"Shall we go and sit down?" she asked.

"Mmmmm."

She sat astride him but not before removing her top. Usually the sight of breasts, beautifully encased in a small white bra, would have had Taylor's crotch swelling. After so many drugs, however, his member remained flaccid and disinterested. It sat dormant inside his pants as they kissed, cuddled and fondled. Sex was still very far from his thoughts.

They were immersed in one another as the club raged on around them, the chemically charged carnage ebbing away as they became lost in their own world. This went on for a blissful eternity, time now having no meaning as they rubbed and kneaded each other affectionately. Skin tingled excitedly as itching fingers wreaked havoc with their senses. The rushes were deep and powerful, coming directly from yearning hearts that shuddered excitedly with each and every magical touch.

Taylor's window into heaven was suddenly shattered by a third party who appeared out of nowhere and sat with them. She was a brunette whose name came and went through Taylor's head without taking root. He felt gutted as she made small talk, unwilling to believe that it was all over. He needn't have worried. Before long she had her arms wrapped around both him and the other girl, alternating her lips between the two of them as he sat there dumbfounded.

Taylor's concentration was cyclical. Sandwiched between intense bouts of intimate touching and kissing was the deeply distressing fear that these were in fact two men. He was too far gone to be certain. A wee fondle here and there reassured him that they were female, yet that nagging doubt remained. He was almost certain they were girls. Almost.

Using his sight helped very little. The Elephants he'd double-dropped caused periodic loss of vision. The acid was also making everything decidedly odd. He couldn't be certain of anything. The girls (if that's what they were) appeared to be merging into a Siamese twin, one that possessed countless tentacle-like limbs that slithered around his body and face like an octopus. Four eyes became eight, then sixteen, as though he was confronting a giant arachnid. The changing coloured lights inside the club caused their skin to glow and halos to form above their heads.

The whole place was jumping now as clubland entered that twilight hour. The atmosphere would build up and up and up until, at 3am, the music would suddenly stop, the lights would come on and security would begin the task of turfing everybody out. Until then the magic was spellbinding and unbreakable, each and every pilgrim immersed in the wonder of it all. All well and truly up for it.

"Fuck aye, motherfucker!" yelled one lunatic, a pale, shaven-headed freak with a massive alien-head tattoo imprinted on one arm.

"Go on yersel!"

Others stood motionless, their limbs as tense as they could make them. Somewhere near the back a horn could be heard. And a whistle. Near the front a girl held an enormous teddy bear above her head. Another was dressed as a fairy.

For Taylor the dance floor might as well have been on another planet. His night was now all about these girls. His personal girls. All that communal togetherness, that incredible symbiotic relationship of great drugs, hard tunes and crazy people that he loved so much meant nothing to him now. Powerful urges to dance and cavort were forgotten as fingers and tongues worked their way around his craving body. All he wanted to do was hold them. Touch them. Feel them.

Life became a timeless wonderland. The situation was so frantic and yet he felt so calm, so wonderfully at peace. It seemed as though they had been together for hours. Perhaps forever. It was probably nearer fifteen minutes.

Then, as abruptly as they had arrived, Taylor's girls disappeared into the crowd 'to dance'. He felt crushed as they vanished from view, leaving him to pick up the broken pieces of his evening. Arduously he raised himself onto trembling feet. A huge weight bore down on him; a heavy forlornness he knew not how to dispel. From head to toe the gold his body had once been was now lead. He wanted to cry. Then, as beautiful as the Holy Madonna herself,

Taylor saw JP standing a few feet away, rocking slowly on his heels, wheeling his arms in a circular motion as though he were cranking up an invisible aircraft that would transport him up into the sky.

"Wuuuuuuuuuh!" he cried, his face lit up like a Christmas tree. "Come ooooon!"

He saw Taylor and gave him a telling nod before embracing him. Taylor began to come up again. His recovery was helped further by JP, who thrust a pill into his gob.

"There's still nearly an hour to go," he announced. "Fucking class!"

Taylor grinned inanely. All the drugs he had taken that night reactivated inside his brain and across his revitalised body. His vision clouded swiftly as the tunes whipped around him in an audio tornado. He swayed uncontrollably, hands waving limply, eyes dilated. As it all became too much for him he emitted a long, protracted sigh and hung onto JP as best he could.

"Aaaaaah!"

"I know mate, I know."

"I'm soooo fucked!"

The memory of the girls was fast disappearing as the drugs regained control of his senses, casting out his melancholy. And still the rushes kept coming. Every inch of him throbbed as he kneaded himself, releasing fresh sensations across his trembling skin. He felt free, unrestricted, no longer bound by the society outside these four walls. Inside everything was beautiful, perfect and pure. This was postmodern culture at its current zenith. Previous generations had talked of 'free love'. This was artificial love. Synthetic stimulants and manufactured music: the choice of a new generation.

Taylor's hands rapidly criss-crossed each other above his head, his verbal diarrhoea now translated into semaphore as he threw shapes at the ceiling. He was flying yet his legs could hardly move. His psyche faded in and out of reality as the minutes ticked by. Moments of unerring clarity, during which everything seemed clear and calm, punctuated the muggy daze that was now his normality.

He managed to raise himself for the final tune, which the DJ respectfully reloaded. He briefly mustered a few shouts and some half-hearted leg and footwork as his hands continued to flutter around his face. And then the lights came on.

BANG!

DOWN...

Down...

Down he fell as demands for "one last tune" went unheeded. The realisation that it was over slapped him across the face. And then did so again. That was that. It was tidy-up-time. The bell was ringing.

He walked wearily towards the exit, hoping for a time machine science had not yet invented to deliver him back to eleven o'clock. As he dragged himself across the rapidly emptying dancefloor, the phoenix of opportunity rose majestically from the smouldering ashes of his night. Standing before him, smiling and beckoning him, were the girls. His girls.

The first girl approached him, hugging him warmly. The other hung back apprehensively.

"What are you doing now?"

"I've got to get my coat from the cloakroom."

"That's cool," she soothed. "We'll be upstairs, we've got to find the rest of our friends."

The cloakroom queue took an age and Taylor feared his opportunity slipping away from. Upstairs, however, he found his girls sitting at a long table. The table was also occupied by other clubbers; miscreants from the dark side. The type that only came in to view when the lights went on. Thirty-somethings with scars and scowls. They were all on happy pills, their jaws gave that away, but they were still miserable and aggressive. People who were always down even when they were up. They surely couldn't be with his girls?

"What's happening?" asked Taylor hesitantly.

"We're waiting for our friends," replied the first girl sweetly.

She had a posh accent and both the girls seemed well-to-do. Definitely English students. There was no way they could be accompanying the half-dozen darksiders. Unless, of course, they had latched on to this dangerous crew as a consequence of some misguided drug adventure they were currently undertaking. Taylor was too wrecked to have a clue either way. He just wanted to leave, preferably with his girls, as soon as possible.

Thankfully the friends soon arrived in the shape of two more pretty English girls. Taylor welcomed them cautiously, trying to suss out if they were latched onto the others while avoiding eye contact.

Before he had time to properly ascertain the truth his vision became blurred and contorted shapes of colour began forming beneath his eyelids.

"Are you coming back to ours?" asked one of the newcomers.

Taylor was unable to make out her face properly and offered a wonderfully apt "…em…" before gurning and shuddering as an unexpected rush bent round his body. He also partially nodded his head and this proved sufficient under the circumstances.

It was just about clear to him that the girls had no relationship with the others sharing the table, though he still had a deep and burning desire to rid himself of their presence. He could almost feel himself being sucked into their grimy universe through some mysterious radge vortex that would see him battered and penniless come sunrise.

The first girl leaned close to Taylor and whispered in his ear, "my girlfriend isn't very happy."

"Why not?"

"Because I pulled you."

When the girls decided to depart, Taylor shuffled along behind them at a safe distance. They were discussing important matters. At the main door to the club, however, a bottleneck of wandering zombies formed and Taylor found himself standing right behind the conversing girls.

"Do you want him?" asked the girlfriend.

"I think so," replied the other.

"Okay."

The chill air outside provided a welcome relief from the closeness of the club and he began to breathe more easily. The girls debated Taylor's prospective sexual career as he surveyed Calton Hill, which was eerily dark and steep, conjuring up fantastic images from books he'd read as a child.

After a time the girlfriend sidled over and announced, "We'd rather you didn't come back with us, sorry."

They left promptly.

Taylor concluded that he had to hastily find the mates he had disregarded for most of the night and searched frantically amongst the groups of people conglomerating on the pavement. They were nowhere to be found and so he made the short walk to JP's flat and an attempted resurrection.

JP's muddled face appeared from behind the door and beckoned him inside. Taylor went straight to the bathroom, which was scabby, dirty and in need of repair. In that respect it was in line with the rest of the flat. Taylor's attention was immediately drawn to the toilet cistern, which had melted. Or was that the drugs? He wasn't sure but the centre seemed to have folded in, leaving a gaping hole and marshmallow periphery. Fearing the trips were playing games, he surveyed the wreckage carefully, running his finger over the edge of the crater. The toilet had most definitely melted. It was the first plastic toilet Taylor had ever knowingly encountered.

Cleaned and refreshed, Taylor entered the enormous living room, which served as the heart of the never-ending party. Each and every couch and armchair, and there were many, had been stripped of their original coverings and were covered in manky throws. Badly nailed together pieces of wood and exhausted metal springs revealed themselves from beneath scanty fabric. From the larger items of furniture cavernous holes spewed masses of flammable foam and sawdust. Once-pristine coffee tables were festooned with rubbish as cans, bottles, but mostly smoking paraphernalia, covered everything. Dank liquid, tobacco and ash coated much of the carpet. Thousands of tiny balls of rolled-up paper dotted the landscape, as did beer bottle tops, empty cigarette boxes, and broken lighters. The air reeked of fine skunk, giving the musty cave a sweet aroma. The room was reverberating to banging acid trance. Taylor's feet began to tap off the carpet. Things were looking up.

JP's flat had four bona fide residents but generally housed at least twice that number at any one time. Life in the flat revolved around the resident dealer, the activities he undertook and the bizarre characters with whom he was acquainted. Known as the 'Sasquatch' on account of his sheer gigantism, he was well over six foot and brawny to match. He was currently sprawled across an entire couch, shirt and shoes discarded, his enormous limbs extended as far as they possibly could. The Sasquatch had a hygiene problem brought on by drug overuse and the sloth such a lifestyle engendered. Basically he stank. He also had the bizarre habit of constantly pinching himself while jerking his back and shoulders violently. These contortions were induced by what he had affectionately dubbed his 'bubble', which he claimed travelled around his body under the skin causing him no end of irritation.

"So what does it actually feel like?"

"It doesn't feel like anything. It's a bubble."

"What sort of bubble?"

"A bubble bubble."

Seeing the Sasquatch dance was a rare event. He usually sat at the side snorting ketamine, which he dubbed 'acid in a shell suit'. He was presently comatose, barely able to interact with the rest of the room beyond the passing and receiving of joints that constantly came his way.

It wasn't long before Taylor was quizzed on recent events. He launched into a typical spiel, fabricating and exaggerating with gusto to the assembled crew

"I was so fucked I couldnae tell if they were birds or blokes! I kept worrying they were you!" he exclaimed, gesturing to Wayne, a Scouse dealer known to swing both ways.

"Cheeky bastard!" replied Wayne, grinning. "Fancy a line?"

Taylor almost fell over backwards as it shot up his nostril and into his already buzzing head. As he twitched his nose agitatedly, a blizzard of powdered snowflakes fell to earth. The chemicals made their inexorable journey down his throat and into the pit of his empty stomach. His teeth tingled as he ground his jaw, his belly now rumbling nauseously. His head reeled and violent jolts shuddered through his limbs.

"Fucking hell!" he remarked, taking a long swig of beer.

One by one, the soldiers took their marching powder. Chatter spewed forth. Everything and nothing was discussed as individuals randomly remembered, released, and then forgot the jumbled-up thoughts and images inside their heads. Some were left lost for words, staring blankly into space, puzzled by how quickly and easily everyone in the room could forget what had just been said. It was as though a tide had swept in and washed away all memory, leaving a bare beach where once conversations had been constructed.

"Mind that festival we went to a couple of months back?"

"The one out at Ingliston?"

"Aye."

"That was fucking mental!"

"Totally! Blue triangular Mitzis!"

"Dog's fucking bollocks!"

"Is that what youse got that night? We ended up with those smacky pills."

"The brown speckled ones?"

"Yeah. Fucking awful, spent most of the night hanging onto my bird, could barely see or anything."

There was talk of hiring a generator, grabbing some sound equipment and heading off to a beach. Someone mentioned a quarry party. And there were the ubiquitous demands for a pint in the Old Salt. But it was all just bluster. The next day could only be put off so long.

Taylor found himself staring bleakly into a half-full mug of red wine, his mind a whirl of empty thoughts. The newspaper on his lap, which seemed to have appeared from nowhere, refused to be read as he furiously scanned the print that danced before his eyes in a desperate last attempt to stay awake. It was no use. He downed the booze and closed his eyes. As the city awoke, he fell into a deep, dreamless sleep.

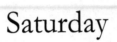
Saturday

At first sound. Muffled. Garbled. Unidentifiable. Then a vague feeling of movement and commotion. A brief opening of the eyes unleashed an unsustainable amount of light. Taylor immediately closed them. Still the noise and movement persisted. The sounds were becoming increasingly audible – the low roar of traffic, a hissing that could only be cooking, and the intolerably loud clumping of feet. There was also a stench in the air. Stale and foul like an old tramp's coat. And a feeling of stiffness and immense exhaustion that spread from head to foot. Another brief burst of light revealed little except that someone was moving around the room. This was confirmed by the rasping sound of a lighter, which was soon followed by the earthy scent of hashish.

Taylor opened his eyes once more and blinked furiously, contorting his face as he did so. At first all he could see was the appallingly dirty floor his head was dangerously close to. By the time he turned his head the person in the room had left, leaving only a trail of smoke by the door as proof of their presence. The chairs and sofas in the room now lay empty; those who lived in the flat had crawled to bed, the rest leaving to find theirs. Only one body remained, lying face down on a bare mattress in the corner, snoring heavily.

Taylor rubbed his face and yawned. He felt compelled to do nothing yet the situation demanded immediate action. At least standing up and getting out of the room, which was causing him to feel ill. His desire was to sleep or at least to lie down somewhere warm and comfortable. But not here and his own bed was miles away. He could not face a walk of any kind.

Somewhere in the back of his mind a thought of some importance was trying to break through. His brain wanted to tell him something. Eventually it did and Taylor was faced with the stark reality that was his Saturday afternoon. He had to go to the football. On a comedown.

"Fuck!"

His first port of call was the bathroom, which in the light of day appeared even more squalid and vile, the melted toilet all the more incredulous. Washing his face, Taylor was faced with his reflection in the mirror. His pupils were huge. Under his eyes the skin was a bruised and dirty purple tone that spread out in large semi-circular rings. Like he'd been punched. The rest of his face was pale with a touch of jaundiced yellow to it, his waxy skin drained of all healthy colouring. His jaw appeared to be larger and more prominent than normal, as though some wicked elf had stretched it in a vice while he was asleep. He looked like someone who had taken a lot of drugs very recently.

He was in no state for the pub, having to chat with older guys he hardly knew, staring into his pint glass as his body melted into the beer-stained carpet. Not to mention the match itself. He couldn't even bring himself to think about that.

The bus crawled through the busy town. It was warm and sweaty and noisy on board. As soon as Taylor got on he wanted to get off again. He wanted to go to bed.

Princes Street was packed with shoppers. Thousands and thousands of them, scurrying like ants from one shop to the next. Taylor half-watched them through the cracks between the fingers that covered his face. He couldn't think of a worse activity to partake of on a Saturday. Except watching the Huns on a comedown.

A bet was a necessary part of his Saturday ritual and he nipped into William Hill at Haymarket. Inside was the familiar reek of tobacco smoke, the floor littered with broken dreams as others were forged at the counter.

As he mulled over his gambling options, Taylor also surveyed the other punters. At the counter a frantic man who must have been a painter, judging by the white flecks on his hair and overalls, was throwing wads of twenties at the cashier.

"Ye'll have tae hurry," she informed him. "It's away tae start!"

"Pit it aw on Beggar's Chance," he replied. "Should be three eighty there."

Standing by the fruit machine was a huge black man wearing a long businessman's coat and a tailored suit with a silk handkerchief in the breast pocket. He stared intently at the dogs from Romford, a slip in one hand and a cigar in the other. As he puffed on the Cuban, Taylor noticed a Rolex watch twinkle under his sleeve.

Those around him were less salubrious. Playing the bandit was an inbred creature with a peculiarly large forehead and ears that protruded from his head like satellite dishes. As he held, nudged and spun, his scrawny and very young girlfriend whined for them to leave, occasionally leaning down between complaints to attend to her baby, which was troubled by all the smoke. After several interruptions to his concentration, the young man turned to her and shouted "Shut it or I'll skelp ye!"

The door opened and a red-nosed pensioner entered. Several similarly aged men greeted him, one with a purple nose shouting "Catterick's aff!"

"What?"

"Catterick's aff!"

"Catterick's aff?"

"Aye, Catterick's aff."

The others agreed that Catterick was off and then returned to watching Doncaster.

Taylor handed his slip to the woman behind the counter, watching jealousy as the man in the suit received a fistful of notes, which he stuffed into a crocodile skin wallet. As Taylor left, Beggar's Chance came in second having lost by a nose.

In the street legions of Rangers fans spilled out of Haymarket train station, serenading bystanders with an ode to Bobby Sands, the Republican hunger striker who had starved to death in 1981.

Could you go a chicken supper, Bobby Sands?
Could you go a chicken supper, Bobby Sands?
Could you go a chicken supper, you filthy fenian fucker?
Go a chicken supper, Bobby Sands – you fenian fuck!

One of them held an orange and purple scarf above his head emblazoned with images of King William of Orange and proclaiming in block capitals: ULSTER IS PROTESTANT. As the previous song died out he sparked another.

Oh no Pope of Rome,
No chapels to sadden my eye.
No nuns and no priests,
Fuck your Rosary beads.
Every day is the 12th of July!

Further on, two youngsters had flags draped around their shoulders and hanging down their backs like superheroes' capes. One was the banner of Ulster with red hand and crown, the other a Union Jack.

Next to them and quite possibly their fathers were two Scotsmen wearing England shirts. One started shouting "I'd rather be a darkie than a Tim." The other clapped along.

Taylor kept his head down. Although Huns generally meant his kind no harm, he was always worried in their presence. The Ardmillan Hotel would bring sanctuary and yet he felt nervous as he reached the entrance, knowing he would soon be surrounded by relative normality. Never a good thing with eyes as wide as dinner plates.

The Jambos

The Ardmillan was full of Hearts fans. Jambos. Some jostling revealed Mikey and Johnny, his mates since any of them could remember, sitting at a table near the back. Joining them was an older friend, Stevie, now beyond his twenties and with a family of his own, and his father, Derek.

"Saw some radge Huns on the way over," remarked Taylor. "You forget just how scummy they are until they come calling."

The men nodded their heads in agreement.

"Thing is Taylor," explained Stevie. "These days you only get the cream of the scum. They used to bring twenty thousand through to Tynie. These days they only get four thousand tickets."

"Cream they may be," replied Taylor. "But they're still scum."

"Nothing's really changed," remarked old Derek sagely. "Same old Old Firm."

"Were things no a lot more civilised in your day?"

"Not at all! Aw these people that say things were better in the auld days are talking pish! Half of them were oot fighting wi' razor blades and bike chains after the dancing!"

He continued, "I mind the '56 league cup final against Celtic. Back then there would have been a hundred and thirty thousand folk at Hampden, fifty for the Hearts, eighty for Celtic, likes. We were in the Celtic end but it was aw mixed in those days. We won 3-1 and after the third goal went in aw the Celtic fans started heading for the exits, throwing their bottles back over their shoulders, no caring who they hit!"

"Did youse see the weather on the telly this morning?" asked Mikey.

"There's severe weather warnings right across the north. Basically everywhere north of Perth is getting it tight!"

"I saw it on the BBC," replied Johnny. "Tourists are being told to leave the area. The roads are packed with folk trying to get out. They interviewed this German family, had come over in their caravan. It nearly floated away! And there was this grumpy bastard and his wee laddie, both Scottish, moaning like fuck. The guy had to be a Hun – fat miserable bastard!"

At quarter to three the lads left the pub. Stevie and his father remained for another pint. They hadn't made kick-off since the mid-eighties. By the time they got inside the stadium the PA system was already belting out the Hearts song.

Away up in Gorgie at Tynecastle Park,
There's a wee football team that'll aye make its mark!
We've won all the honours in footballing art,
And there's nae other team tae compare wi' the Hearts!

Their seats were three rows from the back, giving them an amazing view not only of the pitch but also the beautiful city skyline. The walk was quite a hike and not for those suffering from vertigo. Taylor felt faint and stopped for breath halfway up, just as the teams came out.

Hearts entered the arena first, dressed in their traditional maroon shirts and white shorts. Three sides of the ground rose in appreciation, cheering and applauding loudly.

"Come on the Jambos!"

The blue-clad visitors filed on next. The Rangers end was a sea of red, white, blue and orange. Rolls of toilet paper flew from the stand and onto the pitch, and ripped-up tickets were tossed into the air as though confetti. Giant flags unfurled: Union Jacks, St. George's Crosses, Red Hands.

We are Rangers, super Rangers!
No one likes us, we don't care!
We hate the Celtic – Fenian bastards!
We will chase them everywhere!

The roar from both sets of supporters reached a deafening crescendo as Rangers kicked off. Most of the crowd were still on their feet, shouting, gesticulating. Taylor hauled himself into his seat where he slumped exhaustedly.

Hearts had the better of the opening exchanges, turning Rangers backline with long diagonal passes. A marauding attack down the right-hand side resulted in a corner, which was whipped in at pace. The defence was static, the goalkeeper helpless. The lads were already on their feet, their arms outstretched in celebration as a Hearts player came in at the back post. Trapped in a prison of bodies, the goalkeeper could do no more than twist his neck to watch the ball connect with the attacker's head. His contact was poor and for a moment it spun in the air, unsure of where to go as thousands looked on in anticipation. As though lifted by an invisible hand, it finally flew up and over the crossbar, floundering like a fish out of water on the roof of the net.

"Ooooooooh!"

"How the fuck did he miss that?"

"Useless cunt!"

Hearts soon wasted another chance. A long punt was poorly cleared, the ball dropping nicely on the edge the area. The striker snatched at the chance, however, smacking the ball into the ground and over the crossbar.

"That's fucking pish!"

"Murder!"

"Couldnae hit a barn door!"

Buoyed up by their team's good fortune, and perhaps sensing a backlash once the storm was weathered, the away support burst into song, the entire stand jumping up and down to the tune of 'The Great Escape', punctuating the last note with an ebullient "Rangers!"

"So, what did you guys do last night?" asked Taylor as a Rangers player belted the ball out for a throw deep inside Hearts territory.

"He was shagging!" said Johnny, pointing to Mikey.

"Was she fit?"

"She was alright, aye."

"Tell him the story," continued Johnny enthusiastically.

"Well, it was a bit of a mad night. I was up at Whynot wi' Barry 'n' you ken what he's like after a few."

"Being a tit?"

"Exactly! So, we left around two before he got us a kicking. The bouncers had basically asked us tae leave."

"What was he doing?"

"Just harassing birds and threatening their boyfriends – the usual! Anyway, we git ootside and Barry's singing Hibs' songs, which I'm no too happy aboot. There's some radge cunts, older likes, heading intae The Dome. They were Huns and start giving Barry shit, calling him a Tim, shit like that. Honestly, I had tae physically drag the cunt away, he was trying tae fight four forty year-olds in the middle o' fuckin' George Street!"

"Were you steaming 'n' aw?"

"Fucking blazing, mate, Could hardly walk straight! So I pull Barry away 'fore he gets us leathered, apologise to the Huns for his wideness."

"That's no like you."

"Aye, but these cunts were hard as fuck!"

"So how did you get the bird?"

"We stopped at the Akdeniz for a kebab. There was a couple o' birds in there an' Barry starts laying it on, talking aw kinds o' pish while I'm ordering the kebabs. The lassies are still waiting on pizzas when we get our scran, an' Barry starts munching on his. As he tried tae eat it, and honestly this was one o' the funniest things I've ever seen, a bit o' meat covered in chilli sauce flies up an' lands on one o' the birds, right on her neck. It must have been scalding hot cos the bird wiz screaming wi' pain. Barry disnae show much remorse, likes, starts blaming the Turk behind the counter for making it too hot. This is where I came in. Knight in shining fuckin' armour, helped the lassie clean up the mess."

"And you pulled her?"

"Aye! It was well easy. She was well bevvied'!"

"Where did ye shag her?"

"At her gaff."

"Was she a good ride?"

"Well dirty! I was too reeking tae properly enjoy it, but."

Hearts were once again on the offensive. A swift passing movement saw one of the strikers cleverly draw in his marker, then turn away from him, opening up the space for a shot. He unleashed a venomous low drive that had the goalkeeper flying dramatically down to his right.

"Oooooooooh!"

The crowd crowed expectantly as a wave of maroon swept into the Rangers box for the corner. A chant of "Come on you Hearts" rippled round the stadium as the teams readied themselves.

"We need a good delivery here, Hearts."

"Whip it back stick."

Instead, the taker was unable to beat the first defender with a tame low drive. The ball bounced back at him, but his second attempt was even worse, sailing high into the stand. The Rangers end howled with derision before bursting into song.

It is old and it is beautiful, and the colours they are fine!
It was worn at Derry's walls, Enniskillen and the Boyne!
My father was an Orangeman in the grand old days of yore!
It was on the twelfth that I would wear the Sash my father wore —fuck the Pope!

In amongst them was an incredibly fat man whom the home support baited with a slow chorus of "you fat bastard!". Whole rows of spectators rose to their feet, peering and pointing until most of the ground was standing, their eyes fixed firmly on the man's unsightly form.

> *Who ate all the pies?*
> *Who ate all the pies?*
> *You fat bastard, you fat bastard,*
> *You ate all the pies!*

Rangers soon forced their way into the Hearts penalty area. A desperate clearance landed right at the feet of a Rangers player whose deflected shot was brilliantly saved, the keeper having to readjust his body in mid-dive to flick it round the post.

"Great save!"

"Phenomenal!"

A commotion followed amongst the Rangers fans as fluorescent police officers tried to arrest one of them. Other supporters jostled and sparred with the officers, blocking their path. The offender, a brawny skinhead, was eventually dragged away as the Hearts support chanted "You're scum and you know you are!"

> *Follow, follow, we will follow Rangers!*
> *Everywhere and anywhere we will follow on!*
> *Dundee, Hamilton, fuck the Pope and Vatican!*
> *If they go to Dublin we will follow on!*
> *For there's nae other team like the Glasgow Rangers…*

The Hearts fans responded in kind.

In yer Glasgow slums, in yer Glasgow slums!
You rake in the bucket for something tae eat,
You find a dead rat 'n' you think it's a treat!
In yer Glasgow slums!

A man in his forties clambered awkwardly onto his seat and conducted the crowd from his precarious vantage point. His faded denim jacket bore all manner of Anarchist patches, sewn-on decades earlier and now faded into obscurity. His grey mop was cut into a semi-mullet that had probably been a brightly-coloured Mohican back in his heyday.

You are a Weedjie, a dirty Weedjie!
You're only happy on Giro day!
Yer ma's a stealer, yer da's a dealer!
Please don't take my hubcaps away!

Attention quickly returned to the pitch as Hearts launched an aimless punt upfield. There seemed no danger at all but the ball slipped impudently under the defender's astonished boot and set a path for the Rangers penalty area. A race between the defender and a fast-thinking Hearts forward was won by the latter who collected the ball and charged in on goal. The Rangers player galloped back and, leaning in on the attacker, was able to force him wide. The striker was still able to get in shot with his left foot but the angle was too tight and the keeper saved low to his left.

"Ooooooooh!"

The ball spun into the middle of the box. The crowd held its breath, the goalkeeper now floored and helpless. Having made an opportunistic and lung-busting run from inside his own half, a Hearts midfielder was in the perfect position to slam it into the empty net. This he did with suitable aplomb.

One-nil.

"Yeeeeeeeeeeeeeeeesssssssssssssss!"

Quivering hands touched the sky and hollers became lost in the squall of sound that swept its way around the ground. Old and young cavorted and danced in the aisles, grabbing madly and lustfully at each other. Thousands of people all going completely mental. This is why the lads went to the football. This is why they spent hundreds of pounds to sit through dull, meaningless games in the freezing cold. For that thirty second rush a few times a season.

H-E-A-R-T-S,
If you cannae spell it then here's what it says -
Hearts, Hearts, glorious Hearts,
It's down at Tynecastle they bide.
The talk o' toon are the boys in maroon,
And Auld Reekie supports them with pride!
This is my stooooory, this is my song,
Follow the Hearts and you can't go wrong!
Oh some say that Celtic and Rangers are grand,
But the boys in maroon are the best in the land!

Hearts now had an unlikely lead and the fans milked the moment, chanting their way to halftime.

And now the end is near,
We've followed Hearts from Perth to Paisley!
We've travelled far by bus and car,
And then again, we've been by railway!
We've been to Aberdeen,
We hate the Hibs, they make us spew up!
So make a noise, the Gorgie Boys –
Are goin' to Euuuuurope!

The stadium rocked.

To see HMFC,
We'll even dig the Channel Tunnel!
We'll go afloat on some big boat,
And tie our scarves around the funnel!
We have no fears for foreign players,
Like Rossi, Bonair, or Tardeeelli!
While we're overseas, the Hibs will be –
In Portobeeeeelly!

The second half did not start well, however. Rangers were on the front foot from the off and Hearts could barely get out of their own half. Colour drained from the lads' faces, particularly Taylor who had a headache and was beginning to feel nauseous. Everyone knew the inevitable was on its way. They'd been here so many times before. It was only a matter of time. Rangers were going to score.

Hearts responded with persistent fouling. With a quarter of the match still to go, a defender went too far. Having already been cautioned, he scythed down the Rangers left winger. He pleaded his innocence but to no avail. The outcome was a deserved second yellow card followed by the dreaded red. The Huns behind the goal chanted "cheerio" as he plodded disconsolately from the field of play.

"That's a fucking scandal referee!"

"You cheating west coast bastard."

With the home side reduced to ten men and Rangers already in the ascendancy, the odds were now well stacked against Hearts furnishing the lads with a victory and a celebratory night on the town.

In the main stand things were boiling over, especially those in section N, which always simmered. A few blew their tops and scrambled for the away fans by the corner flag. The police were immediately on top of them, some appearing from the shadows wearing motorcycle crash helmets. In the melee something flew onto the pitch, striking the linesman on the back of the leg.

"Looks like a vodka bottle."

"Mad bastards!"

"There'll be an inquiry. Guaran-fucking-teed!"

The siege of the Hearts goal continued unabated, the side in blue now permanently camped in the Hearts half. The fans spurred the home side to try harder and one player in particular took this to heart, clattering a Rangers striker. The physio rushed on, magic sponge in hand.

"How's your brother, Taylor?"

"Still the same miserable cunt!"

"That lad needs a ride, Davey."

"Fuck, he's no the only one!"

"And how's your course?"

"Shite. I've an essay due next week. Russian

politics."

"How much have you done?"

"Fuck all. Still, no probs, will just get fired into the Pro-Plus, pull an all-nighter."

"I'm sure Duncs tanned a whole packet of them once and went off his nut."

Johnny started laughing uncontrollably.

"Tell Taylor that story."

"What story?"

"The one about the reporter."

Mikey's eyes widened and he too fell into hysterics.

"Duncs used to play for some junior team, cannae mind which. Some shithole oot west. They were playing a big game, cup final I think, and there was this bird reporter there covering the match for the local paper."

"And what happened?"

"Apparently she's a dirty, dirty bitch. Fat dog, likes, but dirty as! They were aw getting bevvied after the match and she took four of them roond the back o' the clubhouse, sucked them aw off!"

"Shut up!"

"I swear tae God, man!"

"Tell him the rest," encouraged Johnny, wiping the tears from his eyes.

"One of them, the keeper I think, was reeking and I mean reeking! She was giving him a gam an' he just lets fly, spunks aw over the place!"

"Aaaaaaw!"

"It went aw over her, aw over his team-mates – everywhere! Then – and this is the best bit – before they can even say anything the boy starts pissing tae!

Piss 'n' spunk…"

The conversation was cut short by another attack. The Rangers left winger, the ball glued to his toe, breezed past his marker and headed for the byline. Just before the ball went out of play he wrapped his foot around it and fired in a wicked cross. The Huns rose to their feet, a rush of noise engulfing that end of the ground. The cross was a yard or so behind the striker but this mattered not. Turning his body expertly, he flung his left leg over his head and executed a perfect bicycle kick. The ball flew into the top corner as the keeper dived despairingly.

One-one.

The Huns roared their approval. Taylor buried his head in his hands. Johnny rocked back in his seat and shook his head wistfully like an old-timer who'd seen it all a thousand times before. Mikey was less philosophical and, after the initial shock, stood up and hurled abuse at the Hearts players for their inadequacies.

"Every time, every fucking time!"

In the middle of the stand, down near the front, there was a commotion. The lads climbed onto their seats to get a better view. A brawl appeared to be underway, between who wasn't clear, and security personnel were trying to break it up before things got out of hand.

"What's going on?"

"Just some Hun in the wrong end."

"Hope they fucking lynch him!"

Lee

The first steward on the scene waded manfully through the throng and placed a forceful hand on the man's shoulder.

"I'm afraid I'm going to have to remove you," he explained politely.

The crowd hissed and spat like a nest of cobras, demanding more than mere removal.

"Kill the fucker!"

"Lock him up 'n throw away the key!"

The offender offered no resistance and continued to direct the Rangers' chorus with chubby fingers as he was led stumbling out of the stand by the steward and a supporting cast of police officers.

With the situation now being handled by uniform, the steward returned to his position pitchside. Standing with his back to the match, he surveyed the crowd for any signs of trouble. His supervisor, miked-up and marching with an air of authority, patted him on the back as he passed.

"Good work, Lee. We're gonna miss you!"

The feeling wasn't mutual. Lee wouldn't miss anything about his brief sojourn into the world of crowd control. He was counting down the seconds until he could hand in his fluorescent jacket.

Stewarding matches had given him few opportunities to actually watch the games. Over six foot, well-built, and exuding the self-confidence of somebody who could handle himself, Lee had been a perfect candidate for all the more difficult jobs. Whenever there was a battle he always found himself in the frontline, leading by example.

Lee's final match wandered towards a draw. As always, the fans took an age to leave, filing through the exits with the docility of cows in an abattoir. Eventually, he handed back his jacket for the last time. There was a slight swagger as he exited the stadium. The swagger of someone with better things ahead of him.

Gorgie Road was a sea of detritus and he stepped carefully around broken bottles and scrunched up chip papers. The reek of horse manure and sweet-scented hops combined with the slightest whiff of damp autumn to create an earthy stench. Glimpses of the future occupied his mind as he covered the short distance home. An impish smile broke out across his face.

The streets buzzed with the anticipation a Saturday evening brings. Not quite as good as a Friday with the seeming infinity of the weekend ahead but good enough all the same. Even in the drab grey climate of a Scottish October people were moving with that little bit of verve the expectation and alcohol aroused in them. For others that verve had already become a slurred stagger and as Lee reached Lothian Road, three Hearts fans were bundled into the back of a police van.

Lee's Tollcross flat was a palace of understated beauty. Everything was functional and attractive, purposeful and organised. Plush pine floorboards reflected on smooth chrome and glass. The soft lighting was as comfortable on the eye as the black leather chairs were on the body. The flat was also spotlessly clean.

A phone call confirmed that his arrangements for

the evening were unchanged. He had some free time and so, as he always did, Lee slipped into his Lonsdales and turned his attention to the assortment of weights in the bedroom. House music played low through his Bang & Olufsen as he bench-pressed earnestly.

Training was like meditation to Lee. It induced in him a transcendental state of physical and mental harmony, all other thoughts blocked out by the relentless rhythm of movement. Exercise and the pursuit of physiological excellence had been the focal point of Lee's daily life since his teens, a routine so ingrained it had become instinctive and necessary. A day without running, swimming, lifting, or some other form of workout, and he felt somehow incomplete. Lethargy would set in, his muscles and tendons wilting like flowers deprived of sunlight. He needed to exercise. It was his addiction. One of his addictions.

Lee had married the needs of his spiritual well-being with those of his financial. He worked in a health club. This allowed him to earn money doing what he loved best. Working out and encouraging others to do likewise was so enjoyable that Lee woke up every morning relishing the day ahead. He loved his work and it showed. His dedication, energy and enthusiasm brought many rewards. Soon he would be manager. He practically ran the place already. Still shy of thirty, that was quite an achievement with so many of his peers still finding their feet in whatever career they had fallen into.

His workout complete, Lee readied himself for the night to come. First he washed thoroughly, rubbing Paco Rabanne shower gel into every pore of his machine-tanned body. This was followed by an extensive hair-removing mission and the application of Molton Brown deodorising products. He then clipped his nails and rubbed the soles of his feet with a pumice stone. Finally, his golden curls were artistically sculpted with Trevor Sorbie gel into that of a surfer in mid-wave.

To cover his buffed-up shell, Lee had an extensive selection of designer garments. Tonight he opted for a pair of Prada Sports, dark Hugo Boss trousers and a light Armani shirt. Smart, simple and effective. A dash of XS on his neck and wrists and he was out the door.

Parked outside was Lee's pride and joy. A boy racer since his youth, a little over a year ago Lee had finally managed to obtain a car to match his ambitions. The vibrant red livery of his Golf GTI screamed guile and speed. The elegant spoiler and gleaming alloys were as distinctive as the racing seats and chrome rally gearstick were serious. This car told the world it meant business before it even revved-up. And when it did everyone knew about it. The engine was as powerful as the body would allow without blowing off the bonnet. At traffic lights she growled masterfully, her paws stroking the tarmac impatiently. A flicker of green halogen and she was off, the phenomenal acceleration leaving any would-be challenger dizzy in her slipstream.

Occasionally he would head out to West Lothian, his old stomping ground, where he could always find willing adversaries. Sometimes they even queued-up, waiting to outpace each other on deserted country roads. Cosworths, Imprezas, Supras, GTOs – Lee had come up against just about every make and model worthy of challenging his beast, and had won every time. Losing just wasn't in his vocabulary.

The drive to meet his date was more sedate. A few years ago he had come close to losing his licence after a succession of needless and dangerous manoeuvres. Losing that would be like losing a limb and he always kept his racing urge in check until beyond the bypass.

At a set of traffic lights in Morningside a squad pulled up alongside. Their vehicle was a Vauxhall Astra done in two-tone. The female passenger likewise. Happy hardcore blared from the sub in the boot. The whale tail clamped to the back was as out of place as the tacky racing stripes along the body, and yet they complemented the inhabitants perfectly. Written on the side of the vehicle was 'On A Mission Under Suspicion'.

The girl wound down her window and leaned over. She spat a lump of gum from her shimmering pink lips and bawled "Let's fucking go then!" The lads in the back nodded in agreement, gesturing as though about to fight. The peroxide driver looked Lee's way, his eyes sparkling.

"Nice paint job," offered Lee. "Your motor looks like an old slag! My wheel trims are worth more than that whole fucking rust bucket!"

As the lights changed the Astra's wheels scorched the concrete beneath them. The engine roared into life as amber became green. For a split second Lee reached aggressively for the throttle but then recoiled. They weren't worth it. He watched the rave mobile speed off in a cloud of dust, the crew whooping loudly as they went.

Tonight's date had been a regular at Lee's work for a few months now. She joined to 'lose weight' even though there was none to lose. Like so many insecure women she was unaware of her own desirability. Until she met Lee. He pushed the right buttons. Relentlessly. After weeks of wooing and what some females might call harassment, she reluctantly agreed to dinner.

She wasn't the sort to offer herself to just anybody, if anybody at all. There was no easy route, no quick fix. Lee accepted from the start that this flight of fancy would be long-haul. It was now five weeks since he had shown her how to use the equipment. Tonight was their first date.

There had been a kiss. Just one. Brief and so unexpected. She had immediately pulled away, blushed and departed hurriedly. Lee thought that was that but two days later she returned and made a date. All his hard work had paid off. Tonight was the night.

Lee had never visited her house before. Having dinner at women's houses wasn't normally how he conducted his rendezvous. This had been her suggestion, however, and he was happy to play along, make her think she was in control.

He parked round the corner from her suburban home. A curt beep indicated his pride and joy was secure and he set off in pursuit of his conquest. The anticipation was beautiful. A barrel full of excitement finished off with a pinch of fear. Just a pinch. Lee had done this so many times before it was routine. Second nature.

As he opened the gate the curtains twitched. Before he had a chance to ring the bell the door opened and he was whisked inside.

The first thing that struck Lee was how beautiful she looked. She was wearing a stunning low-cut black dress that boasted every curve she had to offer. Carefully selected jewellery bedazzled the eye, her flaxen hair perfectly styled earlier that day. All totally over the top. The second thing that struck him was her nervousness. He could almost smell the fear. He liked that. It put him in a dominant position. The hunter role confirmed, he sat nonchalantly on the couch, flashing appropriately timed smiles as she rushed around in a flustered state. Getting him a drink, a hitherto simple procedure, became a bamboozling task

"A Coke? Diet or regular? Sorry, I don't think we've got ice. Would you prefer a tall glass?"

Lee revelled in her confusion. She had been thinking of him all day, all last night, all the day before. She had clearly thought of little else for days.

Lee was his naturally cool self. Everything was just as it should be, just as he wanted it to be. The architect's blueprint was once again a masterpiece of his own design. She wanted him. Now it was time for her to submit to her desires.

"It'll just be a few minutes. It's pasta. Do you like pasta? It's a new recipe," and her eyes momentarily sparkled with hope. "I've actually not tried it before so I hope it's okay..." her voice trailed off as she disappeared into the kitchen.

A second later she was back, fumbling in the CD

rack.

"What music do you like?"

"I really don't mind at all. You choose. Surprise me!" The look in his eye caused such a stir that a plastic case slipped from her grasp and onto the deep-pile carpet. She retrieved it, quickly turning away to hide her scarlet cheeks.

As she left to check on the food, bland easy-listening music leaked from the speakers behind Lee's head. He had no idea who it was mumbling along to the tacky piano chimes. It was before his time. Dinner was fortunately served before the music was on long enough to really irritate him and they moved through to the dining room.

Dull landscape paintings hung on the walls, several tacky wooden carvings cluttering the mantelpiece of a now disused hearth. An immaculate lace cloth flowed from a long dining table, an elaborate candelabra separating two places set with fine silver.

As she brought in the starter, Lee settled himself in the chair at the head of the table. He pretended not to notice her worried expression as he did so.

On a crescent shaped plate were several small fried objects. They smelled fishy. Apart from that there was nothing to indicate what they were. Lee didn't like this. He distrusted food he didn't understand.

"I love Mediterranean food," she said as she seated herself.

Something clicked. Tapas. Lee had seen it when he worked for a summer in Ibiza.

"Absolutely," he lied. "These look wonderful!"

Lee was not a food person. He had no interest in nouvelle cuisine, or any other type of cuisine for that matter. Food was fuel; designed to give the body what it needed to function. Optimum performance required exactly the right balance. Protein, carbohydrates, fibre, vitamin A, B, C: that was food to Lee. His diet was based on oiling and firing the engine inside. Taste and presentation were irrelevant. Everything Lee ate served a physical purpose. It was calculated not cooked, prescribed not prepared. Unknown quantities such as these upset the equilibrium, disrupted the routine. Still, the rewards would be worth the inconvenience.

"You must have eaten a lot of this food when you were in Spain? These won't be as good, I'm afraid…"

"Don't put yourself down," and he slid a chunk of something into his mouth. "Mmmmm, delicious!"

It was rubbery and oily, with bits that stuck between his teeth. Swallowing was a real effort but he managed it. Another followed, and then another, until his plate was clean. With each mouthful he intonated a manufactured expression of satisfaction.

"I must admit that I spent most of the time with British people. All they ate was bacon and eggs, that sort of thing. It was really difficult to find good local cuisine, you know?" He sought agreement, which she offered readily. They were both on the same wavelength, even if he actually wasn't.

"I managed to find a little taverna in the hills."

"Really?"

"It was run by this old couple, lovely people. They made the simplest dishes seem so exciting, so unique."

"Mmmmm. Did you manage to get any of their recipes?"

"Sadly not. They said I'd have to kill them first!"

She giggled as his eyes came alive once more.

"I like to try new things, even if they don't turn out so good. My…" she stopped mid-sentence. "I'll get the main course."

She rushed to her feet and swept out of the room.

If the tapas were incomprehensible, the pasta was uninspiring. For a start it was overcooked. In her haste she had boiled it too early. Now it was clingy and heavy, lumping together into doughy balls. The sauce was sparse and a sickly green colour, sprinkled with what look like bird seed.

"It's linguine. With fresh pesto," she explained tentatively. "I made the pesto myself."

Lee had no experience of pesto. Whatever it was he didn't like it. But that didn't stop him commenting on how difficult it was to make.

"What ingredients did you use?"

She rattled off a few funny sounding things he'd never heard of. He could imagine her poring over the pages of glossy women's magazine, eventually coming up with something that resembled earthworms covered in moss.

She continued with the Mediterranean theme, feeling secure that it was something they could discuss. Lee was happy to smile and nod his way through her ramblings as he chewed the pasta. He was aware, had always been aware, that they had nothing in common. Nothing except their desire for one another. Nothing that she could say would be of interest to him, except to remember and use to get what he wanted. To him she was boring and unimaginative. A woman he could almost take pity on. Her life was an empty void. There was nothing there. That's why he was.

She was becoming relaxed and confident now. His blasé attitude put her at ease, his natural magnetism drew her to him. She toyed with her hair and fluttered her lashes as the small talk flowed. The wine helped too. As he was driving, Lee could only have one glass. Once open, though, someone had to finish the bottle and she was doing a pretty good job. The time was drawing nearer. The moment would soon be at hand.

She was an attractive woman. Not stunning by any means, but worthy of a second glance. He could imagine that once, some years ago, she had been the belle of the ball; the girl all the men craved. A long period of neglect had sown the seeds of doubt in her mind. A night like this would re-affirm a belief in herself she had long since misplaced. She would wake up tomorrow invigorated, reborn. A new woman in every sense.

Lee swallowed down the last mouthful with yet another pretend smile as his hostess toyed with the last few threads of pasta. He could read her thoughts, sense her feelings. She was drawing things out, prolonging her own agony as she deliberated and justified. Having brought him to this table, she was now meekly fighting the forces that had urged her to do so.

Lee watched impassively and in silence, the

chatter having long since ended. There was a tension that could be grasped. Allowing her to dangle could only go on so long though. He would be a fool to leave her be long enough to talk herself out of it.

"That was delicious."

She snapped out of her trance.

"Glad you liked it."

Her smiles were forced and even the most subtle of her movements were exaggerated. She couldn't bring herself to make eye contact. When their eyes did meet it was by accident and hers ran for the cover of the dinner plate.

"Would you like dessert? I've a delicious chocolate cake, though I must admit I didn't make it myself."

"Really, I couldn't. Maybe later. Why don't I help you with the dishes?" he asked casually, moving to get up.

"No, really, it's alright. I'll do them."

It was too late. Lee had already ghosted over to her. His hand reached for the plate, brushing ever so slightly against her arm, no more than a whisker. She flinched and he would have seen a look of complete shock on her face had he not been standing behind her. He lifted the plate slowly as she turned her head as far away from his piercing gaze as it could be. When she looked round again he was gone, a tap now running in the distance. She poured herself some more wine, uncomfortably fidgeting with her hair as sips became gulps.

"Where's the washing-up liquid?" Lee called.

"Wait, I'll come and help you.

The wolf licked his lips.

"Sorry, I should really be doing this."

"No problem, it's the least I can do."

He could almost see the goosebumps bulging on the bare flesh of her arms.

"It's just in here," and she bent over to open the cupboard under the sink. The hem of her dress rose up ever so slightly as she arched her body. Straightening up, her hand nervously pulled it down.

"Here you are," and she passed him a plastic bottle, now unable not to look at him.

He unfastened the cap and squirted the green liquid into the hot, steamy water.

"You wash, I'll dry," and he handed her a dishcloth, again their skin touching ever so slightly.

She waited as he plunged his hands into the water until his forearms were coated with suds. He ran his fingers lightly over the surface as she tried not to watch, caressing the smooth porcelain between his fingers. Each item was massaged tenderly. He passed them to her with his hands and with his eyes. As she dried them off, a most mundane and routine task, her hands trembled.

Before she knew it, Lee had her in his arms, the wooden spoon and towel she was holding dropped to the floor as he slid around her. A moan passed her lips as he gripped her tightly, pressing his solid torso against her breasts. For a moment she was lifeless, paralysed, a helpless maiden in the arms of a vampire. But as he held her close to him she came to life, running her fingers over him as he devoured her.

They kissed one another in a blind fury, tugging and pulling madly. The intensity made her giddy and she swayed violently, rocking from side to side as he explored her lips and neck with his tongue. Nails and teeth tore at his skin, her legs slinking around his hips as he grinded against her.

He had her naked in seconds, bent over the sink and panting. She was so aroused he was inside her without really trying. She shuddered and emitted low howls as he took her. The sex was more frenetic than passionate. Two animals satisfying themselves.

They dragged each other upstairs, Lee lifting and pinning her to the bed in one movement as she clung to him. Lee's prowess with women extended into the bedroom and he rarely left them disappointed. He could tell she hadn't had anything like this in a long time, if ever. She was completely his. For the next couple of hours anyway.

At the height of passion, Lee's attention was drawn to a wedding photo on the dresser. He paused for a second, his gasps turning to a semi-smirk. It took all the effort he could muster to prevent him laughing at the gormless kilted fool looking back at him.

"Is something wrong?"

"No, nothing."

Lee's had his first brush with other people's extra-marital sex in his early twenties. With his best friend's mother. Bored with straightforward encounters, affairs soon became the norm. Most men his age looked for a ring on a woman's finger when they first met her. Lee was no different.

Tonight was yet another notch on his bedpost. She was so keen it almost scared him, her claws drawing blood as she tore at his six-pack. They were

112

so engrossed in each other they didn't notice the sound of the car pulling up outside. Nor did they hear the scrunching of feet on the front path. It was only when the front door slammed shut that the situation dawned on them. At least on her.

"It's my husband!"

"Fuck!"

In all his years of shameless adultery Lee, had never been caught in flagrante. Now there seemed no chance that he could maintain that record as feet thudded ever louder on the carpeted stairs. Voices set alarm bells ringing. For a brief moment they looked at each other, stupefied. Then Lee pulled away and hurriedly bundled up his clothes and shoes. The drop to the back garden wasn't so far, aided by a drain pipe. He scrambled to open the double glazing.

In a flash his belongings were lying on the wet grass. Still completely naked, the hero of our time swung onto the drainpipe and shimmied to the ground just as the door handle turned. The first thing her husband saw upon entering his own bedroom was Lee's bare backside disappearing through the open window.

As soon as his feet touched down Lee swept up his garments and sprinted across the back green. He burst through the gate and into the middle of suburbia, everything exposed for all to see. The street was deserted and he slid his clothes over his body swiftly, the beat of his heart the only sound. He clambered into his car, stuffed the key into his ignition and sped off.

Once the exhilaration passed, a relaxed smile rose

like the sun on his face. He'd done it, enjoyed it, and got away with it. He caught a glimpse of his face in the rear-view mirror and winked instinctively at himself. He whistled his way back into town.

At a set of traffic lights a taxi pulled up alongside. The driver, gloom etched on his ruddy face, cast the whistling Lee a dirty glance and then promptly stalled as the lights changed.

Paddy Donnelly

"Cunt!"

As usual the driver had had a shit night and it was getting worse. They always did. Now he had a fare in the New Town and was already running late. He continued to mouth expletives as he restarted the engine

When he arrived, two respectably dressed young men escorted their strikingly beautiful girlfriends into the back of the cab. Students no doubt. The New Town was overrun with them. All full of themselves and their daddy's money.

Paddy moved in different circles. Hailing from across the water, he dabbled with the Provos back in the day, was a degenerate drunk and brawler, and had been in prison for this, that and the other. The jail was a second home. Not the sort of person the sane and reasonable wanted to come across on a dark night. In every city taxi drivers carried with them a certain, often undeserved reputation. Patrick Donnelly was that reputation. Only a forged licence kept him in a job.

As they drifted through the traffic, the group chatted loudly about dinner parties. Paddy kept his eye on the females, the vile thoughts he conjured up only briefly interrupted by images of beating their boyfriends to death.

Paddy's last stint inside was three years in the Scrubs for rape. He couldn't remember much about the incident except that he had been drunk and she had come onto him. A day later the police were kicking down his door. At least that's how he recounted it to anyone who asked.

Having disgorged the cab's contents outside a swanky bar, Paddy drove over to South Bridge where a crowd swarmed outside the Festival Theatre. The first to reach him were a couple in their early sixties. Well dressed and well spoken. The gentleman was sprightly for his age, resplendent in a dashing dinner jacket and tailored overcoat, and sporting a fine silver beard. His wife wore an elegant blue dress. Silver jewellery flashed and sparkled in the streetlights, complementing her well-dressed hair of the same tinge. Paddy expected a tip.

"Have you been to the theatre this evening?" he asked, putting on the politest voice he could. He sounded like an Irish country gent. The type who wore tweeds and owned racehorses.

"Yes, yes we have," answered the gentleman.

"Did you enjoy it?"

"Very much so. It was a modern adaptation of Julius Caesar. Very well done."

"Really?" Paddy enthused. "I don't get to visit the theatre so much these days, what with the job and all."

Paddy hated the theatre. It was full of queers and ponces. And English bastards. Or so he'd been told. He'd never actually been.

"We can't get along as often as we would like either," replied the lady. "What with our social commitments."

"I see," said Paddy, not attempting to ask what those were. There were limits to the details he would allow himself to converse on.

"The two of us are very much involved with the National Trust for Scotland," she continued. "And

Charles is chairman of the local botanists' society."

"How interesting," replied Paddy through gritted teeth.

The taxi pulled up outside a beautiful mansion of a house, just as Paddy had expected. He took the unusual step of holding the door open for them. A tip was dispensed. Sizeable enough to justify his gentile façade.

Using his extensive local knowledge, Paddy weaved his way through as many back-roads and side streets as the geography of Edinburgh would allow, avoiding heavy traffic and speed cameras. He had a booking over in Colinton. Miles away.

The fare was a mother and her young daughter. Both seemed anxious, the woman close to tears. They were heading for the infirmary.

Paddy listened intently as the two conversed.

"Is Daddy going to be okay, Mummy?"

"Yes, Sweetheart. Yes he is."

She looked far from convinced, mascara smudged, nose sniffling.

"How did he get hurt?"

"Mummy's not sure, sweetheart. An accident."

"What kind of accident?"

"Mummy doesn't know."

There was a sterner tone to her voice.

"Why not?"

"The hospital didn't say."

"Is Daddy going to die?"

"No...no. Of course not!"

Her voice trembled with fear.

"No, everything is going to be just fine. You'll see."

"But what'll happen if Daddy dies, Mummy? I don't want Daddy to die!"

The little girl was now hysterical.

"He's not going to die!" her mother screamed back.

She reddened with embarrassment as she caught Paddy's eye in the mirror. He looked away.

Paddy remembered the passing of his own father. His had been a long time in coming, worn away by a persistent tumour. Paddy had only been a child then, newly arrived in Scotland having escaped the Loyalist mob that torched their family home. Dark days.

At the infirmary, a raised hand and shake of the head indicated that payment was not necessary. On the way out he nearly scraped a passing ambulance, offering only a one-fingered salute by way of an apology.

Outside Anderson's bar on Lothian Road he acquired a couple of degenerates. She had a worn face, at the centre of which were two black eyes, narrow and sinister, that appeared dead save for a malicious spark that lingered in the shadows. Tight clothes covered a wiry physique. Her crimson lips lacked the ability to smile except in manic anger.

The man wore a stained polyester suit that had undoubtedly been worn in court earlier that day. His face wore the classic glaikit Scottish expression: dumb and questioning.

Paddy noticed them arguing as he pulled up and, once in the cab, they were immediately at each other's throats again. The sort of domestic disputes that ended in a bloody dead heat, the police scratching their heads as to what to do.

"Ah telt ye no tae fuckin' dae that!" he ranted.

"Wha'? Wha'? Wha' did ye fuckin' tell us?"

"Ye ken fine well, ya fuckin' bitch!"

"Dae call me a fuckin'…"

"Shut it!"

"Hey!" she piped up. "Don't you iver tell us tae shut it!"

They were now eyeball to eyeball.

"In fact, dinnae tell me tae dae fuck all, ya fuckin' cunt!"

Spittle flew in all directions.

"Dae ca' me a cunt, ya fuckin' slut!"

Paddy had yet to ascertain what the dispute concerned. It seemed unimportant to either of them, the conversation having progressed on to drunken insults.

"Yer a fuckin' stupid cow, ye ken that? A'ways fuckin' moanin'. A'ways stickin' yer fuckin' nose in!"

"You kin fuckin' talk, ya big-moothed cunt! Yer jist a…"

"Shut it, Ah've hud enough!"

"You've hud enough?" now very loud. "I cannae…"

"Excuse me, could you two please stop?" interjected Paddy as politely as he could. "If you want to fight you can do it in the street!"

The man flashed an angry look in his direction but the woman stepped in.

"Aye, aye, sorry! See Dode, the man disnae wanna listen tae yer shite!"

"Ma shite? Why ya fuckin' bitch!" and the man slapped her hard across the face.

Paddy again asked them to desist. The response this extracted was less than cordial.

"Just fuckin' drive, ya prick!"

That was enough. A line had been crossed. Paddy slammed on the brakes and the taxi screeched to a halt. Grabbing his jacket, he stormed out into the cold, damp street. He wrenched open the door on the man's side, just about tearing it off its hinges.

"Get the fuck out!"

"Oh, ah see! Think yer fuckin' hard, dae ye?" The man postured, ready for action.

"Aye, think yer fuckin' hard?" mimicked the woman, standing by her man.

Paddy didn't say a word, instead revealing from inside his jacket what could either be described as a small sword or a very large knife. It was, in fact, a bayonet from the Great War. Paddy kept it on the passenger seat, under his jacket, for special occasions.

The smooth, polished steel gleamed in the streetlight. The rain dripped off the raised blade like blood.

"Do I have to repeat myself?"

Bravado evaporated, the couple stepped apprehensively onto the pavement. Paddy quietly wrapped up his weapon and got back in the taxi, giving the two of them an arrogant smile as he sat back in his seat.

"If I see either of you again I'll cut yer fuckin' heads off!"

Before he had a chance to calm down, three young stooges flagged him down. Two of them were wrapped in oversized jackets, one Timberland, the other Tommy Hilfiger. Denims and hiking boots completed the ensemble. A blue and white collar poked out from under the Timberland's jacket. Paddy instantly recognised it as the shirt of Glasgow Rangers. This sight ratcheted up his anger another notch. Paddy hated Huns.

Sitting between them was an older, shaven-headed youth wearing a knee-length leather jacket, smart trousers, black polished shoes and a designer shirt. He clearly thought he was the man and, displaying facial scars and an eyebrow piercing, probably was in certain circles. Black and blue protruded from under his shirt collar, suggesting a full-torso tattoo. In one paw was a large bundle of tens and twenties that he was counting furiously. In the other was a mobile phone, cupped to his ear.

The taxi pulled up outside a tenement on Leith Walk. The Hardman instructed Paddy to wait and got out with Hilfiger. The Hun stayed put.

"So you're a Rangers man, then?" asked Paddy after a couple of minutes, nodding at the lad's shirt.

"Aye."

Paddy rolled up his sleeve, displaying a grand tri-colour tattoo declaring the sacred year of 1916 and threw the Hun a stare that would have turned Medusa to stone.

"Well ah'm fuckin' no!" and he grinned, revealing a single, scary gold tooth.

The Hun gulped and looked away. Paddy roared with laughter, settled back in his seat and whistled 'The Fields'.

When the Hardman and Hilfiger returned, Paddy couldn't help noticing a package bulging from inside the Hardman's jacket pocket. A plan hatched in his brain.

"Right mate, just take us up the Cowgate."

Paddy laughed and, slamming his foot to the floor, sent the cab hurtling in the opposite direction. The three stooges at first looked bemused, then shocked, as the cab swerved violently in and out of the traffic. The Hardman tried to gesticulate but a dangerous right onto Brunswick Road caused him to fall out of his seat.

"Ya fuckin' prick! Ah'm gonnae fuckin' kill ye, ya fuckin' cunt!" he bawled, apoplectic.

Near Easter Road, down by the old railway line, was a collection of derelict factories and warehouses. Abandoned since the war, these last remnants of Scotland's great industrial past were seldom visited except by vagrants and spray-can wielding adolescents. In the city yet out of the way. Nice and quiet. Ideal.

Paddy pulled over next to a dormant warehouse. Every one of the windows was smashed, leaving slivers of glass scattered amongst the debris. The area was eerily quiet, as Paddy had expected it to be. There were no streetlights. No noise. Nobody.

He parked the taxi flush against the wall of the building, rendering one door inoperative and leaving the three goons with a single means of escape. Moving quickly, he blocked this with his giant frame.

The Hardman remained unimpressed and, as Paddy opened the door, motioned to him, his jaw jutting out and his fists raised.

"Fuckin' come ahead!"

With an idle flick of the wrist Paddy re-seated him. Blood spattered the inside of the cab. The effect on the Hardman was like having the guts ripped out of his body. He looked pleadingly at his assailant, all bottle having been comprehensively shattered by that single, decisive blow to the face. A blood-stained tooth slipped from his mouth and onto the floor of the cab.

"Look mate…what is it ya want?"

"That package of yours for a start," he answered, gesturing towards the bulge in his coat.

"Okay, no problem!"

Slowly he reached for the package, then slipped his hand into the other pocket and produced a small but deadly flick-knife. He smiled with satisfaction as the blade popped out.

"Yer gettin' fuck all fae us ya radge fuck! Now were gettin' oot o' here…and if you try anythin' ah'll fuckin' stab ye!"

Paddy shook his head.

"You fuckin' doughballs!"

In one fell swoop he knocked the blade into the darkness, grabbed the Hun, who was sitting nearest to the open door, and dragged him out of the cab. Roughly holding the urchin round the throat, Paddy eyeballed the Hardman with a glare of fatal determination.

"Give me yer shit or I'll break his fuckin' neck," he stated slowly and coolly, mayhem dancing in his ice-blue eyes.

Silence followed, the only sound being the Hun's whimpering, until the Hardman eventually tossed Paddy the package.

"That wasn't so difficult, was it?"

He released the Hun from his chokehold. The boy promptly collapsed and threw up down the side of the cab. Streaks of yellow sick streamed out of his nose amidst hysterical crying. The other two got nervously out of the cab, watching Paddy's every move. He growled ferociously at the Hun, now whimpering at his feet.

"Look what you've fuckin' done, ya wee shite!"

He turned to his standing companions.

"I'm Paddy Donnelly. You'd do well to remember that. Now fuck off!"

They bolted.

"Now you, ya Hun fuck! Yer gonnae have tae clean this up now, aren't ye? Take off yer jacket."

After a startled pause he did so. Hurriedly.

"And that fuckin' rag," gesturing toward his replica shirt.

Wet and freezing, the boy was forced to clean his own vomit off the cab door with his Rangers shirt. Paddy chortled.

"Hey, you missed a bit, ya Hun bastard!"

The boy shivered as the wind chilled his naked torso.

"That's all it's fuckin' good for, ya Proddy fuck!" chuckled Paddy, standing menacingly over him until the job was done to his satisfaction.

"Now fuckin' beat it!"

Clutching his jacket and filthy shirt, the skinny wretch scampered off into the night.

Paddy surveyed his haul. It was pills, neatly stacked in little white pillars of ten and tightly bound with cling. A couple of hundred pounds' worth. Not bad for fifteen minutes' exertion.

Paddy's next fare was over in Meadowbank. His instructions were to get over there as soon as. No other details were given. He revved up the engine.

He reached the address in no time at all. Before him was an incredible sight. Scattered across the pavement were numerous articles of clothing, books, toiletries and CDs. All lay dirty and damaged on the wet tarmac. More items rained down from an upstairs window, landing in the gutter or bouncing off nearby cars.

A distraught man scuttled around in his pyjamas, desperately trying to collect up his belongings before the elements destroyed them. The more he tried to hold, in both hands and under each arm, the more squirmed out of his grasp and landed back in the muck. There was also the added concern of being hit by the frequently flying debris, some of which seemed to be aimed directly at him. He would glance up sporadically at whoever was orchestrating this mayhem, occasionally offering futile cries of dissuasion.

"Please stop! We can work this out!"

Paddy watched from a distance for a good five minutes a good five minutes, enjoying the spectacle, before the man noticed him and ran over. Paddy got out.

"What's going on?"

"It's my wife, she's chucking me out!"

"Well you can't just put all yer shite in my cab. There's regulations 'n' that!"

Realising that his fate was now in Paddy's hands, the man begged.

"Please, I'm desperate. I'll pay you extra. Anything you want, please?"

Paddy mused, then relented.

"Alright, but it'll cost you an extra tenner."

"Fine. Thank you," and the man returned to picking his life up off the ground.

It was then that her upstairs began aerially removing some of the man's more expensive items. First a small portable television flew over their heads. It crash-landed in the middle of the street, glass and plastic flying in all directions as it exploded on impact.

"Nooooooooooo!"

His stereo came next. Bit by bit it took the same leap of faith. Speakers, amp, CD player – all shattered on the unyielding concrete, spewing their mechanical guts across the street. Screaming could be heard from upstairs. Paddy wasn't able to decipher exactly what was being bawled but got the gist. 'Cheating bastard' was one of the more audible terms.

Most of the man's clothes were now safely in the cab, wet but redeemable. Breakable items continued to fall from the heavens, however, and could not be saved. A stylish lamp, a mobile phone, a personal stereo, mugs, glasses, and football trophies, even a guitar that made a curious, musical sound on impact. All ended their days out there in the street.

"So, what did you do then?" asked Paddy.

"I'd rather not talk about it if you don't mind."

"Another woman was it? Been playin' away from home?"

"Her sister," came a meek reply.

Paddy laughed, nodding wistfully. "Always the way!"

His next fare was a drunk and very distressed young woman, barely able to communicate her destination amid fits of wailing and sobbing. Paddy was unconcerned by her plight. He was more interested in the short dress she was wearing, which she kept trying to pull down in the direction of her knees. His mind raced with ideas. Nasty, evil, immoral ideas. It had been a long time.

She was under the influence and tarted up. Probably not even supposed to be wherever it was she had been. What parts she could remember she wouldn't be able to adequately explain. No one would believe her. No one would even care.

Without really even thinking about it, Paddy changed the cab's direction. Back towards the warehouses. The young girl didn't look up at first, still bleating and mumbling to herself. Then, as though struck by lightning, she sat bolt upright and declared that she was going to vomit.

Paddy pulled over. At the third attempt she managed to grab hold of the door handle. As it opened she fell out into the gutter. Thin, soupy vomit spilled from her mouth. Paddy considered dragging her back into the cab when a middle aged couple appeared in the distance. Concerned, the woman rushed down the street to help the young girl. As she gently lifted the girl's head, allowing her to vomit more easily, the man approached Paddy.

"Had a bit too much to drink, has she?" he asked jovially. "Florence Nightingale here'll sort her out. My wife's a nurse."

"Okay," replied Paddy, "but I can't really hang about."

"No bother. We'll see that she gets home alright. Has she paid you yet?" asked the man, reaching for his wallet.

"It's fine. As long as she's alright, that's the main thing."

Paddy did not have long to dwell on this turn of events. A group of men crossed the road, one of them waving his arms wildly above his head, pointing furiously at the cab. Perplexed at first, Paddy soon recognised the miscreant. It was the Hardman.

Paddy gestured to him with a camp wave, his broad face grinning from ear to ear. The Hardman responded by hurling himself clumsily at the vehicle, shouting and bawling at the top of his lungs.

Paddy charged out of the cab and, grabbing the Hardman round the midriff, swept him clean off his feet before smashing his frame violently off the cab's bonnet. Only his agonising cries masked the sickly crack of breaking bones as he tumbled in a dishevelled heap onto the concrete. The others fled, scattering like startled pigeons.

Violence made Paddy hungry. A chippy would go down a treat and he was soon parked up outside his favourite. He was in such a hurry to get his blood stained hands on a steak pie and chips that he didn't notice a group of people standing on the pavement, including a young woman directly behind his cab door. As he got out of the vehicle he bumped into her and she fell awkwardly. He muttered a gruff and wholly insincere apology.

Rebecca

"Are you alright Becks?"

"Yeah I'm fine," replied Rebecca, rubbing the base of her back.

The alcohol had taken away most of the pain, the embarrassment less so. There would be an almighty bruise in the morning but for now only her face turned purple.

"Are we all here then?" bawled one of the group.

"Where's John?"

"In the bathroom."

"Well if he doesn't hurry up he'll be on his own!"

"Oh, shit," cried another. "I was meant to phone Davina. Can I borrow somebody's mobile, I've ran out of credit?"

"No, Lisa, it's okay," interjected another. "I've already spoken to her. She's staying in tonight."

"Really? She seemed up for it when I spoke to her this afternoon."

"You know what she's like. Besides, I think she has to work tomorrow."

"Here, wait," remarked Lisa, rummaging in her handbag. "I think I've left my purse."

"No, Lisa, you gave it to me remember?"

"Oh yeah," and she giggled. "God I'm so drunk!"

Nights on the town. Rebecca avoided them like the plague. Definitely not her scene. She preferred lazing in front of the TV in her pyjamas with a warm drink and a hot water bottle. Or sitting under the shade of a tree absorbed in a good book. Drinking until she dropped, which she was due to do any minute, was not normally her idea of enjoyment.

Her Saturday had begun the same as any other. She awoke as the day reached its sixth hour. Rebecca had no need for an alarm clock. It was inbuilt.

Morning was Rebecca's favourite time of the day. It was the only time she truly had to herself, when she could relax and take things easy. It was also a time of great anticipation as she looked forward to another day. Saturday mornings were best of all; lovely, long hours of freedom and possibility lay ahead of her like an endless horizon. As her flatmates slept, she fired up a pot of fresh coffee. Rebecca liked hers strong and of the highest quality. Her coffee had to be filter espresso that an Italian would approve of. It had to be fresh and aromatic, and with the kick of a demented mule. For until the precious medicine had passed her lips she was merely an empty vessel, void of life and meaning. Her day did not truly start before coffee.

How Rebecca drank her wonderful elixir depended on her mood and the time of day. First thing in the morning, as the sun was still finding its way in the sky, she drank it neat, slugging a shot back like a drunk does whisky.

Her eyes were still half-closed as she ground the beans. But as the aroma wafted upwards she began to wake. She heated the potent blend on the electric stove in a little metal pot she'd picked up in a flea market in Amsterdam. The bottom of it unscrewed to reveal a special compartment where the powder was stored. Like loading the barrel of a gun.

When thoroughly brewed, the mixture was then transported to a dainty wee cup so innocent and unassuming one could be forgiven for thinking it was just an ornament of some kind. In truth, it was the launch pad for a nuclear missile.

There the viscous blend would remain for just a few seconds as the sweet scent filled the room. Then she devoured the mouthful, shuddering with pleasure as it smacked her across the face. The day was now hers to do with as she pleased.

Next was breakfast. And another coffee. Whereas her first cup was a life-giving injection, her second was pure indulgence. As the black gold brewed away, she would heat about half a pint of milk on the stove, keeping the temperature low to avoid boiling it. She had a special metal device for whisking and as she teased the implement slowly between her fingers the milk came to life, frothing and foaming in the pan.

The milk and coffee were then poured into a cup the size of a soup bowl. The smell made her giddy; so deep and yet so light. Two beautiful opposites brought perfectly together. A smidgen of cinnamon dusted over the top added a little extra edge.

For breakfast she always accompanied her coffee with yogurt, this being her other morning staple. She liked to vary what she added to it and this morning Rebecca was particularly fortunate that a mango she had bought nearly a week ago had finally ripened. Every day she had squeezed it ever so slightly in her hand. And every day the fruit had felt like a smooth brick. Today, however, even with the slightest touch her fingers slid easily into the flesh, revealing the juicy interior.

She peeled and sliced it eagerly, cutting right in until the knife scratched every last sinew from the bone. The juice flowed in rivers across the chopping board, and also over her hands and down her arms until she was elbow deep in sweet yellow blood. She mixed the sticky, wet pieces into a bowl of plain yogurt along with the sliced rings of a banana, a sprinkling of Brazil nuts crushed until almost powder, and a handful of plump raisins.

Rebecca curled up next to the window with Dostoyevsky as content as a person could possibly hope to be, only looking up to administer generous helpings of fruit and satisfying gulps of coffee. It was twenty minutes past six.

Being a student of English Literature, she devoured books voraciously and incessantly, chomping through two or three masterpieces a week, her eyes scanning the page at breath-taking speed, each word, sentence, meaning and inference digested in the blink of an eye. From her cosy spot in the kitchen, as the nation idled in slumber, she journeyed the many highways and byways of human imagination, moving nothing but the page, the spoon and her enormous cup.

A little before eight, Rebecca washed up her dishes and left the flat. The streets were bathed in a warm, golden sunshine that belied the nip in the air. It was cold but dry. A clear blue sky suggested it might remain so.

At the west end of Princes Street was a thin sliver of a lane that most folk passed without noticing. This was the back end of Shandwick Place and for every smart shopfront that greeted shoppers on that thoroughfare, this lane housed an old wooden door where staff and deliveries quietly slipped in an out.

Outside one of these doors three people wrestled with a large piece of tarpaulin. A toolbox sat open on the pavement and Rebecca could hear loud banging noises as she approached.

"How's it going?" she asked, instantly feeling the warm comfort of camaraderie and comradeship that would stay with her for the rest of the day.

"We're trying to get the sign ready," replied a man in his forties, who was bent on one knee with a hammer in his hand, scrutinising a length of wood. "But we don't have any nails, just screws."

"A problem!" laughed Claire, a young girl in a multi-coloured jumper. "John's been trying to get it secure for about ten minutes now."

John was visibly losing patience, at both the task in hand and his own failings in relation to completing it. The arrival of Rebecca merely added to the pressure he was now under. With each screw that bent or fell from his grasp his frustration mounted and his masculine pride diminished. Eventually he got one of them to penetrate the wood. It wasn't straight and hardly professional but it would do. The second screw, however, was more troublesome and the onlookers stood in awkward silence until the sign was finally battered into shape.

"Well done, John!"

Relieved, he shrugged off his efforts and returned to business.

"Okay, have we got everything?" and he looked around, taking a mental note of the folded up table and two large plastic boxes sitting by the wall. "Then let's go."

A short while later they were setting their stall at

the far end of Princes Street. Being Saturday it was already busy and even before the flyers were removed from their boxes curious passers-by made enquiries.

"We're fighting for trade justice," explained Rebecca. "Many farmers in poorer countries are being made bankrupt because of protectionist trade policies implemented by the west."

The woman listened intently.

"We're urging people to write to their local MP. Take this leaflet, it will explain what to do."

"Thanks, I'll do that."

Rebecca's morning consisted of various such encounters.

Having volunteered in a Guatemalan school in her gap year, Rebecca found a charity fighting for trade justice within weeks of starting her studies at Edinburgh and began volunteering on their stall. A new world opened up. She met like-minded, intelligent people with whom she could debate and discuss. There was such energy, ideas and visions. She was now part of something positive. In her own small way she was making a difference.

Not everyone saw it that way. Rebecca shared a flat with two other girls, Lisa and Sarah, who were both friends from school. Sarah was domineering, opinionated and rude. Her idea of a good time was to get drunk on vodka and sleep with a stranger. She was everything Rebecca wasn't and from day one battle lines were drawn. Rebecca rarely went out, to the point that the others stopped asking. Going out and drinking was not her thing.

Tonight was Lisa's birthday, however, so there

was no getting out of it. Worse still, all Lisa's friends from back home were coming through for the occasion. Sarah clones who lived in a culture where teenage pregnancy was the norm and conversation rarely strayed beyond nails, hair and celebrity gossip. Rebecca struggled not to look down her nose at them. They treated her with equal contempt.

Lisa had suggested a restaurant, prompting Sarah to immediately book an Italian place that specialised in catering for large groups. "There's a live band," she enthused, handing them a flyer with picture of a middle-aged Italian couple named 'Marco and Maria' and promises of 'a wide selection of Italian and international songs'. As she walked back to flat, Rebecca prayed for intervention, divine or otherwise, that could deliver her from this ordeal.

In the flat were Lisa, Sarah and three other girls. They were already drinking.

"Hi," offered Rebecca meekly. The others replied in kind with only Lisa's face showing any genuine warmth.

"Do you want a drink?" offered Sarah.

"In a bit. I just need to get ready first."

She headed straight for her room, imagining the looks the others were giving one another.

A good while later she was ready, having agonised over several outfits, none of which she enjoyed wearing. Rebecca didn't like skirts or tight clothes. She felt much more at ease in baggy jeans and T-shirts. Clothes she didn't have to constantly pull down or fidget with. Tonight, though, necessitated some effort, if only to tone down the inevitable bitching from Sarah. Jeans and a T-shirt would be savaged.

Rebecca had a long, flowing skirt of beautiful blues and greens that she loved dearly. It was the only skirt she enjoyed wearing. She also had a top that matched it perfectly. Sarah, however, had disparaged it some time ago and she hadn't worn it since. She stood for a while, holding it against herself in the mirror, telling herself to go for it. To hell with Sarah. It didn't matter what she said or thought. But it did. And so she settled for a nondescript black number that showed off too much leg and cleavage for her to feel comfortable in.

"If you like I can lend you a pair of shoes that would go great with that dress?" offered Sarah, knowing full well that Rebeca's feet were two sizes bigger than her own. Rebecca politely declined.

Thankfully for Rebecca, Lisa had invited people from her course and there would be more than twenty of them at the meal. That meant safety in numbers and if she was smart she would be able to avoid Sarah for most of the night.

They all met in a bar near their flat, Rebecca remaining silent on the walk over as her flatmates were updated on who was doing what with whom back home.

"I don't actually reckon it's his. I mean, she said to me only the other month that they never do it anymore."

"I reckon she went home with Jimmy that night but doesn't want him to find out."

"Jimmy? No way?"

In the bar were several friends from university and Rebecca began to relax. She was in better company now. Sarah had also invited guests of her own. Young men who would no doubt vie for her attention until she decided which one she would take home. First in line was a handsome young man who'd come on his own and didn't know anybody other than Sarah but seemed undaunted and was generally charming and friendly. Rebecca's money was definitely on him. The other two were friends who found it easier to chat with each other than interact with the females. Tweedledum and Tweedledee.

Knowing only too well her low tolerance for alcohol, Rebecca wanted to start with something soft but the others were having none of it. Lisa had been given a bright red hat with flashing lights on it, which she donned as a round of Breezers arrived. Rebecca grimaced.

A few bottles later they moved on to the restaurant. It was undeniably and unashamedly tacky. Large columns, grotesque statues, a framed photo of the Leaning Tower, models of gondolas. Every aspect of Italian culture painfully packaged and reduced to meaningless tat. Rebecca hated it.

The others didn't seem in the least bit bothered. Sarah was already making suggestive comments about one of the waiters. Tweedledum and Tweedledee were on the periphery, unfortunately next to Rebecca, and were discussing football. Lisa's hat was still on but only just. Rebecca was concerned by the way Sarah and the others were plying her with drink.

The musical extravaganza was still in the preparation stage as they took their seats: a man in a ponytail could be seen connecting sound equipment at the back of the restaurant, speaking earnestly into a walkie-talkie as he did so. For now there was still no sign of 'Marco and Maria' themselves. Rebecca held her breath.

To add to the sense of occasion, a large and raucous hen party had situated itself at the next table. Old, overweight women dressed as nurses, shouting, singing and accosting the waiters. The tone of the night had very definitely been set.

The restaurant was packed, everyone seemingly there for the entertainment, and people were getting restless. At the entrance to the kitchen, an overweight Italian caricature traded concerned glances with the Ponytail. Eventually, after several exchanges of brow furrowing, he heaved himself across to the sound system. Curses and gesticulating hands followed, though Rebecca was unable to discern if they were genuinely arguing or simply being Italian. After a few minutes the Caricature returned to his spot by the kitchen, assuring the customers that the show was about to start. He was as good as his word.

The couple entered the stage to rapturous applause from the lubricated throng. Each of the performers had seen better days. Marco was undoubtedly wearing a toupee; a black rug that perched on his head as noticeably as that of a judge. A painted guitar hung from one shoulder and over a gaudy silk shirt and trouser combo. Maria cut an Annie Lennox figure with cropped blonde hair and 80s suit. She was the more enthusiastic of the two and engaged the crowd with a series of nods and smiles before sitting herself behind a Casio keyboard.

"Hi, we're Marco and Maria!"

Marco offered a vague acknowledgement as the spectators whooped their approval.

"Before we begin I'd just like to apologise for the delay. We've been having some problems with the neighbours – they've complained about the noise."

Cue pantomime boos.

"We can still perform but we have to keep the noise down. I know, I know, it's not up to us I'm afraid."

Rebecca smirked.

"We've installed a sound-o-meter," she explained through gritted teeth, bringing the restaurant's attention to a small box on the far wall. "The guys here will keep us right and ensure we don't breach any regulations…"

The Ponytail and the Caricature both waved to the crowd.

And so the farce began.

They started with an Italian number. He strummed along on the guitar, his face forcing mechanical smiles at regular intervals. She played the piano well and had a good voice. Too good for these circumstances. Perhaps Marco had dragged her down to his level. Or maybe he had once been talented too but had given up, worn down by doing gigs beneath his dignity. Gigs like this.

Rebecca pondered this thought as the Ponytail intervened, pointing at the flashing red light on the sound-o-meter, much to the annoyance of Maria who immediately moved down an octave. Marco paid no attention and continued strumming along, his half-hearted contribution making little difference to the sound levels.

Conscious of the early hour, Rebecca knew she would have to pace herself but the group were taking so long to order their food and the wine tasted so good she soon found her glass empty before the starters had arrived. By the time they did, Marco and Maria had moved on to modern classics, which they butchered in the wrong key, Shania Twain's 'That Don't Impress Me Much' being particularly painful. Maria tried her hardest but was constantly thwarted by the red light and by Marco's disinterest. The noise level undulated with remarkable haste. She would reach the light-flashing crescendo only to be forced to descend to a barely audible whisper as the exasperated Ponytail swung his arms above his head. The crowd seemed to enjoy it, the farce merely adding to the entertainment value. Even Rebecca found herself smiling and swaying ever so slightly as they launched into Berlin's 'Take My Breath Away'.

The restaurant may have been tacky, the entertainment more so, but Rebecca couldn't argue with the quality of food. She ordered a simple bruschetta as a starter, believing this classic to be a window into the soul of any Italian kitchen. As far as bruschetta went, this one was up there with the best. The wonderful fragrance of fresh basil filled the air even before the plate was put in front of her. The tomatoes were plump, juicy and full of flavour, covering the crisp bread liberally without turning it soggy. There was garlic but not too much, just enough to add depth to the taste without overpowering it. She sensed vinaigrette too but there was no sourness as she savoured her first mouthful. The food also seemed to improve the taste of the wine. As did more wine.

The hen party was now well and truly sozzled, some of them dancing and cheering. They weren't the only ones. People everywhere were on their feet – husbands and wives, young couples, old ladies and their grandchildren. The Caricature could barely contain his delight as he dashed between the tables.

By the time the waiter served Rebecca her wild mushroom risotto, which was both rich and wholesome, Marco and Maria had left the building. Their performance did not culminate in an awe-inspiring encore but rather was terminated abruptly and in bad spirits. Rebecca was no lip-reader but was still able to decipher Maria spitting "I can't work under these conditions" at the Ponytail following yet another red light, before marching off, dragging her disinterested partner with her. The crowd was at first confused, then angry.

"Is that it?" bawled a drunken hen.

"Boooooooo!" jeered another.

The Caricature, whose face now beamed red and was damp with perspiration, placated the hecklers with free wine. Within minutes Marco and Maria were no more than a distant, dreadful memory.

Tweedledum and Tweedledee, shy and uncertain in the company of the fairer sex, had doggedly discussed football all evening. One of the girls in the group, now on her fourth glass of wine, decided to venture in to the conversation. A tedious exchange followed during which the two men positioned various items — glasses, pepper pots, salt shakers — on the table in order to explain the offside rule.

"I don't get it."

Rebecca cringed.

Sarah was enjoying the undivided attention of First-in-line. She smiled coyly, occasionally fluttering her eyelashes at him. She certainly knew what she was doing and was very good at it. Rebecca remained peripheral.

The group moved on to a vodka bar, during which Rebecca took her unfortunate tumble. The bar was more akin to a sweetshop than a public house. Laminated menus and chalkboards offered various, seemingly innocent beverages with names like Honey Bee and Moonshine. Rebecca considered making her excuses but had drunk enough alcohol to entertain the thought of more. She wasn't a fan of the Russian poison but when mixed into colourful concoctions it became bearable. Sarah, who now had her arms locked around First-in-line's waist, was a veteran of this particular establishment and took charge, ordering several cocktail pitchers and a round of flavoured vodka shots. Rebecca was hesitant but, under considerable peer pressure, opted for mango. The drink came in a totsy glass only half-full with yellowy liquid. It smelled fruity and sweet and in no way alcoholic.

"Right everybody," cried Sarah, "one… two… three!"

They knocked back the shots with a swagger. Even Rebecca drank hers in one gulp and was amazed at how easily — and pleasantly — it went down. The same could not be said of Tweedledum who had foolishly chosen chilli vodka in a fit of male bravado. On downing the shot he grimaced painfully, coughed and ran to the toilets.

The pitchers – and there were many – were filled with wonderfully bright and sweet-smelling delights and crammed full of ice. There was creamy chocolate, sharp citrus, sweet strawberry, even bubble gum. The group sampled them all, sipping from their tumblers through party straws. Although they tasted harmless, the cocktails were laced with rum, vodka, brandy, Malibu, Kahlua, Bailey's, tequila and schnapps to varying degrees. They packed quite a punch but one that crept up on the drinker and smacked them around long after they'd let their guard down. Three of the party left before the pitchers were drained. Tweedledee was also absent, searching outside for Tweedledum who had not returned from the toilet.

Rebecca again considered leaving but was enjoying herself too much. Her accident outside the restaurant had earned her much sympathy and even Sarah and her gaggle of witches were being nice to her. She also found them much easier to talk to after a few drinks and was chatting away about celebrity gossip and trashy TV shows, things she hadn't realised she knew so much about.

In the back of her mind was guilt. Not that she was drinking too much and losing control but rather that she was normally so distanced from this life and so condescending of it. At this moment she felt like she belonged, like she was accepted by normal people. Why did this only happen when she was drunk? Was she really so reserved and cold when sober?

"Let's go clubbing!" shouted Lisa, who was still compos mentis albeit practically horizontal.

"Yeaaaah!"

"Whhuuuuuh!"

The club was five floors of sleaze and drunkenness. Everywhere people were far too drunk and far too amorous, this being the last refuge for the Saturday night mentally-impaired. No sooner did they arrive than Rebecca was accosted by a moustachioed, middle-aged man in a tuxedo. She looked on in horror as he gyrated painfully close to her, his eyes sick with lust.

"Hey babe, how are you doing?"

"Clearly a lot better than you!" she replied instantaneously.

Impressed, the group cackled as they pushed passed him.

"What an arsehole!"

Rebecca too was impressed by her own self-confidence and the ability to fire such a retort. This was undoubtedly the drink, of which she wanted more.

The group found their way to the third floor where Abba was belting out 'Dancing Queen'. There could be no better clarion call for drinkers to make fools of themselves. Shameful dancing ensued.

The club was full of hen parties; groups of women in matching outfits cavorting in circles, surrounded by male vultures hoping to pick off the more vulnerable members. Lisa's flashing hat dragged several men into their sphere, the better looking ones welcomed at first, then told where to go once hands started straying.

Rebecca, who normally viewed such scenes with horror, was finding it all very amusing. She also took great hilarity in two flamboyantly gay men attempting to out-dance each other to Madonna. She occasionally joined in, wiggling and shaking her behind.

"You go girl!"

As the night wore on, Rebecca's energy sapped and her head became numb. The boundless enthusiasm ebbed away, replaced by a muggy, hazy stupor. Uneasily, she sat herself in an armchair in the corner and viewed the carnage. The group had dispersed some time since and she could only see Sarah on the far side, her arms and lips wrapped around whom Rebecca presumed was First-in-line. A respite from their passion, however, revealed it to be someone else. How typical of Sarah, she thought, to lead a man on all night only to end up with somebody else. Her brief friendship with her hated flatmate and her entourage was already at an end. The frivolity of a few hours ago was now forgotten as the spirits enveloped her in a cloud of spite. Her passage from sobriety to fun-loving party girl to miserable drunk was now complete. It was time to go home.

Then she saw him.

He was standing at the edge of the dancefloor with a friend. She recognised him instantly, before she'd even caught sight of his face, for he was wearing the same distinctive red shirt he'd worn when she first saw him nearly two months ago. She had already got up to leave but, rather than exit, she returned to dancing as best she could, one eye fixed on him.

Rebecca had no idea why she found this stranger so desirable. No words had passed between them, not even a glance save the awkward and soon forgotten ones people within a close proximity of one another make throughout any evening. She had no idea where he was from, what he did, what he liked and disliked. She didn't even know his name.

She had first noticed The Stranger in a beer garden at the end of summer and felt a murmur in her heart she had not felt in a long, long time. She couldn't explain the reason for this but it was there all the same. He was handsome with a kind face and a warm smile. That this should make her giddy perplexed her and she thought about if often in the intervening weeks. Many men were handsome with attractive features. Why, then, should he stand out? Feeling a great urge to confront The Stranger, to introduce herself and find out more, Rebecca composed herself and worked over in her mind what to say. How should she, one who would never normally be so bold, introduce herself? The last thing she wanted was to come across as desperate. Or cheap. What line would be casual enough to prevent this? What combination of words, out of all the infinite compositions she could conjure, was the right one?

Rebecca considered this for several minutes as she danced, her mind turning over a variety of possibilities, all immediately discounted for one reason or another. Everything was so disjointed, a thousand thoughts racing by too fast to be grasped and pinned down. She was far too drunk and yet only in this state would she ever attempt what she was now planning.

Their eyes met unexpectedly. He turned her way and, as he took a sip of his drink, his dark eyes connected with hers. She nearly jumped and a flush came over her. A slight smile flickered across her mouth. He smiled back, at least she thought he did, and then turned away.

This was it. A sure sign. She had to do something.

As she drifted towards The Stranger, heart in mouth, a most unexpected and intolerably cruel event occurred. A blonde woman appeared from nowhere, smiling flirtatiously with The Stranger before planting a kiss on his cheek. Rebecca could feel herself being sucked through the dancefloor.

Who was she, this tart? Was she his girlfriend or just a friend? Did he want her? Did he love her? Whatever the answer, Rebecca had no intention of hanging around long enough to find out. The uncontrollable urge to weep surged through her and she stumbled away, fighting back the embarrassing tears. She reached the cloakroom with her mascara just about intact. This great sadness was nonsensical, and she fought it determinedly as she handed over her ticket. There was no need to cry, she told herself. No need at all. Yet a few rogue tears seeped out nonetheless.

Ten minutes later Rebecca was in bed. She curled up in a ball, praying the room wouldn't start spinning, her head throbbing as the dull thud of the dancefloor echoed in her ear. She thought briefly of The Stranger but was not awake long enough to dwell on him.

Sunday

Rebecca's head pounded. She wasn't used to hangovers, their rarity making them all the more intense. As soon as she sat up in bed the guilt washed over her. It poured down her back and over her arms and legs in a slick, fluid motion. Memories formed; minute flashbacks, often no more than a glance or a whispered word, even a thought that had never left her head. And yet they dug deep and were as sharp as knives. This feeling would not go away for the rest of the day.

Her mouth was the proverbial rabbit cage. She had forgotten to drink any water before she went to bed, at least she couldn't remember drinking any. In fact, she couldn't remember going to bed or even how she got home. These absences of memory hurt more than the bits she could remember. Stolen pieces of her life during which anything could have happened.

As she crawled out of bed she reasoned that this horrendous guilt was a by-product of the alcohol. A friend once told her that hangovers induced guilt. It was all in her mind. Then she remembered falling over outside the restaurant and cringed.

In the kitchen the sun was streaming through the window and Rebecca withered in a light she would otherwise usually have basked in. She struggled to pour herself a glass of water, her hands shaking as she ran the tap.

This was horrible.

A cup of coffee later she felt little better. The intermittent thundering of jackhammers persisted, as did the constant crawling of the skin. And no amount of water could remove the fetid taste of death from her mouth. No sooner did the cool liquid slip down her throat than her mouth crusted over again. She also felt sick.

From the hall came voices, not all of them familiar. Rebecca moved over to the door and peeked through the gap. She could see Sarah standing by the front door in her dressing gown. The other voice was a man's but he wasn't in view.

"I've got to be making tracks."

"Will you call me?"

Rebecca was struck by the tone of Sarah's voice. Quiet, almost mournful. She'd never heard, never imagined she'd hear her flatmate sound so vulnerable.

"Sure."

He kissed her hurriedly on the cheek and left, Rebecca catching but a brief and indeterminable glance before the front door closed behind him. Sarah made for the kitchen and Rebecca stumbled back to her seat, trying to look surprised when her flatmate entered. Sarah was the more startled, however, and looked sheepish as she poured herself a drink.

"Who was that?" asked Rebecca, pretending to read yesterday's newspaper and bearing the expression of someone who couldn't care less.

"Just a guy."

"What's his name?"

"Kenny."

"How do you know him?" Despite her hangover Rebecca was as cool as ice. This was probably the only time she'd ever see Sarah like this. In half an hour she'd be back to her normal brash and evidently false self.

"I met him last night."

At this point Rebecca looked up and briefly caught eye contact with her flatmate.

"Well I hope you used a condom?"

Silence.

"You did, didn't you?"

"I'm going back to bed." Sarah exited swiftly.

Rebecca left the flat in a strop. She had all kinds of emotions boiling up inside her. There was anger at Sarah for her stupidity, but also pity, and deeper still was a nagging loneliness. And still the guilt persisted.

It was a beautiful day. The previous night's rain perfumed the air, which was warming nicely. The birds chirped freely under an endless blue sky. Even in her present agony Rebecca couldn't help but smile.

She entered Mr Palavar's shop, made directly for the fridge and pulled feebly at its door until it eventually slammed into her. As she reached into the arctic cave her head immediately felt better. Just a little. She paused briefly in the chilled space until the freshness caused her skin to tingle, then grabbed a pint of milk and slammed the door shut.

"Good morning," chirped Mr Palavar. "How are you today?"

"Morning. I'm feeling a bit rough."

He emitted a booming laugh and rocked back a little, his belly wobbling comically as he did so.

"What is the point in being young if you cannot enjoy yourself?"

With a swirl of his arm her attention was brought

to a number of medicinal products living in irony next to the tobacco.

"I am sure you can find something here to relieve your headache. I also hear that Irn Bru is good for a hangover. I would not know for I do not drink," and he laughed again. "I always seem to run out on a Sunday. The worse a state the customers are in the more they seem to buy!"

"No, thanks, just the milk, please."

Rebecca left the shop vowing never to drink again. As she did another customer entered and walked straight to the counter.

Tom

The man looked thoughtful, almost wise, and gave the impression that he was forever in contemplation about one thing or another. His silvery hair flowed in locks around his ears and his face was covered by a rampant beard that masked everything save his eyes, which were bright and such a light shade of green they were almost clear. He was short and slim but with strong arms and rough hands pockmarked with scars.

"Good morning," boomed Mr Palavar. "How are you today?"

The man paused for a second, his attention caught by the pile of Racing Posts stacked up on the counter. "Alright, yeah," he remarked before following, almost as an afterthought, with "Today's my birthday."

"Happy birthday, my friend! And how many years have you chalked up?"

"Too many to recall!"

"Ha ha! I too have reached that age. Every year I take one off rather than add one on!"

The man smiled but offered no further comment and for a second or two there fell a silence that he was perfectly at ease with, Mr Palavar less so.

"So, what can I get for you?"

"Ten B&H, please."

Outside the sun was shining brightly, as it had been all morning. The sky was such a crystal clear blue Tom could be mistaken for thinking it was actually a tropical lagoon or the waters of an exotic sea. There wasn't a cloud to be seen.

Now puffing on a cigarette, he walked so slowly

he was barely moving, his feet shuffling along in a slovenly gait. He wasn't allowed to smoke in the house, which was at the end of the street, therefore necessitating an amble rather than a march home.

He had managed to cut down to two or three cigarettes a day and felt sure that in the coming year he would quit altogether. Quite an achievement for a man who once went through three packs a day.

Tom entered the flat with the stealth of a thief, turning the key as lightly as he could and opening the door with such care that it made no sound. So quiet was he that his own wife didn't hear him until he was upon her. She went to scream but stopped herself, clasping her hand to her mouth. She then smiled and looked down lovingly at the tiny bundle in her arms.

"I thought we could go to the Botanics as it's such a nice day."

"I'd like that."

Jessica was now awake and as he lifted her into the baby carrier she gurgled excitedly.

"Hello sweetheart! We're going to the Botanical Gardens, aren't we? Yes we are! You're going to see lots of exciting things, my little angel!"

Tom and Sue were of modest means and had a vehicle that, while roadworthy, had seen better days. A white Ford Fiesta festooned with bumps. Tom suspected that a previous owner had engaged it in some off-road shenanigans. Inside wasn't much better. The seats were matted with irremovable dog hair, again from a previous owner. The interior also smelled of wet dog. The couple tried to mask the odour with air freshener but it was always there, a lingering reminder of the car's past life.

The gardens were in their full autumn splendour and the trees and pathways were a riot of russet red, flaming orange, burnt gold and yellow ochre that shone in the brilliant glow of the sun. Rich hues exploded all around as nature marched its endless cycle.

Many families had decided to visit and the Gardens were alive with children playing. Love and laughter were all around. As he and Sue strolled hand in hand, Tom thought of their future together and what it might hold, whether they would return here in years to come with Jessica running and playing, perhaps with siblings. Would they even come here with her children one day?

Experience taught Tom never to look too far forward. He tried as best he could to live for the moment, to savour what he had and never take it for granted. That could not prevent a spot of day-dreaming, however, on such a pleasant afternoon and in these picturesque surroundings.

His childhood had been one of poverty. Poverty exacerbated by his father who was drunk more often than he was sober. In the mining communities where he grew up, Tom's circumstances were normal enough. As soon as he was old enough he followed in the footsteps of his father, his grandfather, and presumably countless fathers before them. Life was defined by drinking and fighting. He gambled too.

Cursed by an addictive personality, Tom's life spiralled out of control. The more responsibilities that confronted him, the harder he hit the drink.

Eventually his life imploded and he lost everything to the booze and the betting slip. He fell into vagrancy, wandering the streets of a foreign town, begging and stealing enough to drown his sorrows.

He awoke one morning, very early and just as the birds were beginning to sing. He was lying on a bench by the canal, soaked in his own urine. It was cold but, mercifully in one way, he still had a few gulps of Scotch left to warm him. As he sipped, watching the sun rise, the reddish glow reflecting off the water, a realisation poked its way through the thick alcoholic cloud. It was his 32nd birthday. A great sadness befell him.

The canal was freezing cold. He didn't so much jump in as gravitate inexorably towards it, the stagnant water sucking his body under as the despair had already done his mind. He blacked out immediately from the cold. Nothing flashed before his eyes. There was only darkness.

It was only later, much later, that Tom realised that the feeling of rising with the angels towards heaven was in fact his body being dragged from the murky water by mortal hands.

Bouts of conscious delirium and troubled sleep followed. When awake he was always looking upwards at faces he did not know. Strangers peering at him as though he were a museum piece on display in a glass case. He would snarl and lash out at them, causing them to flee. But he couldn't find the strength to break out of the case and the faces always returned, more concerned and interested than before.

After several days of this, the faces introduced

themselves as a couple called Theodore and Margaret, whose house his glass case was in, and a doctor with a foreign sounding name. The couple had been walking their two red setters along the canal bank at just the moment when Tom had taken the plunge. A minute earlier or a minute later and he would've died unnoticed. It was Theodore who dived in and, being in his early seventies, had almost killed himself in the process. Tom appeared as grateful as he could when all he really wanted was to be dead and gone from this world. And a drink.

His first thought was to get up and leave, and run to the nearest off-licence. But he had no money, not a bean, and so the terrible, wicked idea of robbing the old couple entertained itself inside his sick mind. He was too weak, however, to do other than convalesce in the presence of these kind and generous people.

"Alcohol is one of the hardest things to beat. I know, I was there too once," offered Theodore. "And it's all the harder when you feel that you have nothing to look forward to."

His voice was very middle England. Soft, calm and respectable. Tom responded the only way he knew how.

"What the fuck do you know about me?"

He wanted to grab the man by the throat and strangle out of him every last condescending breath but he was too weary to raise his hands. And so it continued.

"I can help you. We can help you. Like I said, I know what it's like. I made it but only because there were others there to help me through it. If you think there are people who can help you I am happy to contact them. If not, we are here for you. The worst thing for all of us is if you leave here and then jump into that canal again."

"I'd be better off in that fucking canal, believe me. Everyone would be!"

"Why do you say that?"

And with that Tom opened up his heart and soul with a fury, relinquishing a confession that saw him weep uncontrollably in front of this stranger before collapsing into an exhausted sleep. It was the best sleep he'd ever had.

Theodore and Margaret were both retired and able to spend considerable time with the patient as he recuperated. Margaret stayed out of the way most of the time, only entering his room to feed him soup and clear up. Theodore, however, was there constantly, by Tom's side, as he built up his strength.

Tom thought he had Margaret and Theodore figured out from the moment he first laid eyes on them. Wealthy, spoilt toffs who felt guilty about their comfort and saw him as a way to make right the gulf that existed between his world and theirs. And so he decided to milk them, to accept their food and lodgings for as long as they offered but always with the intention that he would throw it all back in their patronising faces when the time was right.

When Theodore and he spoke about life, Tom treated him with mild contempt, as though Theodore were a child or halfwit who lacked the knowledge and experience to be considered an equal.

"You wouldn't understand it, mate, you just wouldn't. No fucking money, fuck all, five of us all having to go out and find food for ourselves."

Then Theodore politely dropped his bombshell.

"I can't pretend to know what you went through but I do recall in the depression, in the '30s, when times were really tough, my mother sending us all out to beg. I was very young but I could see the guilt in her eyes, like she'd failed us. I don't believe she ever recovered from that…"

Theodore, for all the middle class comfort he now enjoyed, was one of ten children. He'd worked for what he had now and he'd also suffered greatly along the way. He and Margaret had two children. George, the older of the two, died of a heroin overdose back in the days when such tragedies were unheard of. Their second child, Emily, had been born severely handicapped, her complicated birth leaving Margaret barren. She died aged seven.

"Not a day goes by when I don't think of them both."

The drink, for all its power, relinquished its grip on Tom after a week or so of sobriety. Not completely, far from it, the drink would never completely let go, but enough to allow him to breathe, to look beyond the bottle. It slipped into the shadows along with the other demons. There it skulked, unseen but not forgotten.

With his new-found sobriety came a new lease of life, a surge of energy that compelled him to act. But Tom had never done anything before. All he knew was the drink. He was faced with a big void of nothingness, a blank canvas he did not know how to paint. Until Theodore introduced him to his workshop.

He was a carpenter by trade and had become very successful designing and producing furniture with an old friend. Together they had built up quite a business, which they had sold several years ago for a handsome profit.

"I have a workshop, not much, just a shed really, but I still like to go out there from time to time and make something. Like your bed for instance. I don't know if you have any experience of working with wood but I can show you, I'd be happy to show you."

Woodwork was the only thing Tom had ever been any good at at school and he'd briefly entertained notions of going to college before the drink took over completely. He'd never mentioned it to anyone. Now he had an opportunity, a golden opportunity, to pick up where he'd left off all those years ago. But the nihilism was still strong, the male pride throwing up the same old barriers.

"Nah, I'll only fucking break something!"

Theodore continued to encourage him but Tom wasn't for budging. He went to bed that night indignant, convinced he was useless and that there was no point. The next day he changed his mind. It was the best decision he ever made.

Theodore's shed was more a barn, with a high, sloping roof that let in the rain and shaky walls dotted with holes. The place was a mess and Theodore looked slightly embarrassed, not having considered how it would appear to others, and began tidying up at random, muttering apologies as he did so. Tom barely heard him, so overwhelmed was he by all the tools and wood that surrounded him. Ideas, wonderful, creative ideas began to sprout in his mind.

The two men spent most of the following few weeks there, Theodore happy to teach his craft, Tom eager to learn. He picked things up quickly, old school lessons soon dusting themselves off in his mind. He had a natural talent and could fashion the wood quickly and effortlessly. Once he mastered the basics various items followed; first some shelves, then a chair, and a small table. He followed Theodore's instructions at first but, as his confidence grew, he added his own signature to the designs.

Theodore was always there, a comforting presence in the background. Except, that is, on Sundays when he and Margaret went to church and Tom was left alone. As soon as he heard the car crunch its way down the gravel driveway, his mind turned to drink. He found he couldn't concentrate on his work, on anything, as his mind and body yearned for alcohol. He was able to fight the urge but only by pacing around the garden, never for a moment settling in one spot. He would pace and pace and pace until the familiar crunch on the path told him they were back. Only then could he relax.

This curse was a great worry to Tom whose mind was straying towards a future away from the elderly couple's hospitality. A future he would spend with himself, most probably by himself, alone with burning thoughts that demanded drink to quell their fires. There had been no discussions on when Tom should leave and the couple seemed happy to put him up indefinitely but he knew that there would come a time when he would have to move on. The prospect terrified him and was made all the more daunting by these swift descents into oblivion whenever he was alone.

On the third Sunday by himself Tom succumbed to the demons. He left the house and hitch-hiked to the nearest town. He couldn't remember anything after that. The next thing he knew, Theodore was bailing him out of the cells.

Tom's conversion happened slowly and unremarkably. There was no brilliant ray of light from the heavens, no sudden realisation. He wasn't born again.

Having been shamed by his relapse, he tentatively asked Theodore, who was patient and understanding in the face of Tom's indiscretion, if he could attend church with the couple. He was no Christian, hadn't set foot inside a church since childhood, and his original motivations were purely for reasons of self-preservation.

"I'll just sit there quietly. You won't know I'm there."

"Certainly you can come," replied Theodore without expressing any enthusiasm. "But I should explain that we're Quakers."

Tom's command of divinity was weak. He knew roughly that Christianity was divided between Protestants and Catholics but he did not know the difference between them save that the latter had a leader who lived in Rome. Quaker was not in his lexicon and as such was an alien and potentially dangerous word to be treated with suspicion. He recoiled and shifted uneasily.

"So you're not Christian?"

"No, no, we are. Absolutely we are. But Quakerism is a branch of Christianity, a lesser-known branch, and we do things a little differently from other churches."

These words only heightened Tom's fears. Religion was weird enough, what with the wafer, the fire, the brimstone and the men in strange robes. Different from that could only mean weirder. He feared that these Quakers were some cult, that he had been brought here by this apparently kind couple in order to be brainwashed. He knew there had to be an ulterior motive to their altruism and now he was sure he had discovered it. As Theodore continued, he was already planning his leave.

"Quakers have similar beliefs to mainstream Christians only our beliefs are more diverse than you might find in other churches. We do not have a priest or preacher in the traditional sense. There is nobody who tells us what we should believe. Our services aren't like masses where a leader directs the congregation from the pulpit. The definition of 'God' varies from individual to individual – we don't all believe in this physical entity, this deity that is all seeing and all-knowing. Some Quakers do not even believe in God at all, at least not in the traditional sense."

Realising that he was rambling, as he was prone to do, particularly on matters that interested him, Theodore paused for breath. Tom didn't know what was going on. The words had washed over him without really sinking in and all he could glean from this speech was that Quakers didn't believe in God. This worried him yet further.

"So what do you Quakers believe in?"

"The main principle that guides all Quakers is that of non-violence. We are pacifists. Therefore our beliefs are as much political as they are spiritual. Throughout history Quakers have renounced violence and campaigned against war."

Tom felt slightly relieved by these words. Although not necessarily in agreement with such a philosophy, it at least fitted with the caring and compassionate people who were currently housing him. It made this group seem less threatening. But still he had his doubts.

"So what happens at your church?"

"Friends meet…sorry, I should explain, Quakers are known as Friends."

Tom continued to look concerned.

"Friends meet at, well, 'meeting'! That's what we call our services. Basically we sit around in an informal group and contemplate. People say prayers if they wish, or not, it's up to them. Afterwards we have lunch together. I don't know what your experience of church is and I appreciate you may find this a little, well, strange."

Theodore was a quiet, private man who had never before explained his faith to someone so completely unaware of it. He tried to put himself in Tom's shoes and explain things accordingly, make them sound as normal as he could. Judging by Tom's face he was failing miserably.

Tom said no more about the matter and threw himself into his craft once more, spending every waking minute sanding and sawing his way through the mountain of wood stacked against the far wall of the shed. When he was in there, working with the wood, he felt completely at peace, oblivious to the world outside, relieved of the burden of his past and the demons it harboured.

But when Sunday came the demons returned. He could feel them as soon as he woke, hovering in the shadows at the end of his bed, hatching plans. They knew that Theodore and Margaret would soon be leaving for church or whatever it was they went to. They knew that once alone with Tom they could overpower him. Tom knew this too and despite having assured Theodore that he would be fine, that the previous weekend's calamity had been a one-off, he began to debate the merits of accompanying them to their meeting. The benefits were obvious. Regardless of what their church had in store, nothing could be worse than the prison, both literal and metaphorical, into which the demons would deliver him.

The deliberation went on for much of the morning as Tom worked a kitchen stool, the rhythm of his movements disrupted by his internal struggle. Sense prevailed and, with a heavy heart, he mumbled his wishes to Theodore.

"I'll just sit there quietly, won't be any bother."

As ever, Theodore was kind and understanding, and immediately set about finding Tom some clothes to wear. He had no garments of his own and was dressed in tatty old shirts and trousers Theodore had long since retired. He could not attend church in such a state and so Theodore provided him with a suit. It was an old, dull, brown colour and by no means a perfect fit with the sleeves slightly on the long side and the trousers dangerously loose and in need of a sturdy belt. Tom also embarked on a hasty and impromptu grooming session, cutting back his unkempt beard and taming his wild and overflowing hair.

Studying himself in the mirror he felt a small and unexpected sense of pride, as men do when compelled to make an effort regarding their appearance. He looked younger and more handsome than he had done in many a year and, more importantly, there was a spark in his eye that had been absent since childhood. He felt alive, purposeful even, despite the fact that he was living off the generosity of strangers, had no worldly possessions, no education or training, and had to be monitored constantly to keep him from the drink. Even in the most barren of places hope could spring forth and as Tom eyed himself in the mirror he felt, for the first time in his adult life, that there was a future worth looking forward to.

Tom's first meeting was an awkward experience. It was held not in a church but a house; a far more intimate setting than he'd imagined. There were about twenty people present, all of whom knew each other. Tom therefore stood out as an interloper and felt painfully self-conscious.

'Meeting', as Theodore had described, took place in an ordinary room, essentially a large living room, with a series of chairs, not all of the same type, arranged in a horseshoe shape. On the walls were a few family photos and a poster for an art exhibition. No crosses, no stained glass, no pulpit. Tom found it all very underwhelming and yet as they took their seats the intimacy stifled him.

The room fell silent, the others sitting with their heads bowed, deep in contemplation. Tom didn't know what to do or where to look and busied himself by fidgeting with his suit, brushing it with his hands and painstakingly removing small balls of fluff. The silence was intense, claustrophobic, and he was soon loosening his clothing as sweat formed on his skin.

Quite unexpectedly, a woman stood up.

"I want to say a prayer for the people of the Balkans who are suffering greatly at present. I pray that the violence will end and that the people can live together in peace and prosperity."

She sat down as others murmured their agreement and nodded their heads thoughtfully.

Tom was stunned by this sudden outburst. He didn't know what the Balkans meant or what violence she was referring to, or what concern it was of hers.

Another person, an elderly man with thinning white hair and a red face, stood up.

"Yesterday I saw a pregnant woman fall over in the street. She was immediately helped to her feet by three people who collected the shopping she had dropped. They sat her down on a nearby bench and comforted her as she was in a state of shock. One of them called for an ambulance as a precaution."

Tom felt very confused.

"I thought to myself that, in a world that is supposedly becoming fragmented, where people are isolated from one another, where there is said to be a culture of mistrust and indifference, people still show great humanity and kindness."

He sat down again.

These words resonated with Tom, even though he was still confused as to why they had been said. He thought of Margaret and Theodore and everything they had done for him. Without them he'd be dead, no doubt. The penny was beginning to drop. These were not religious nuts. They were decent people who drew strength from these meetings.

Another man got to his feet.

"I have read with great concern the worsening situation in Somalia where thousands are without access to food. I call on us to pray for the people of the region and all those currently risking their lives to help them."

Somalia was another word that meant nothing to Tom. He wondered if it was near Romania, though he didn't know exactly where that was either. Tom had always been aware of his ignorance, of his lack of education, but for the most part it hadn't really mattered. The bottle never asked probing questions and demanded no more than the ability to open one's mouth and swallow.

After several more speeches, one of the group shook hands with his neighbour, prompting the others to follow suit. Theodore offered Tom his hand and a genuine, honest smile. Tom returned the gesture.

Meeting ended thereafter and was followed by lunch, the younger members of the group helping to unfold three tables around which the chairs were placed. Bowls of lentil soup were handed out, as were hunks of crusty bread and jugs of iced water. The soup was hearty and tasty, and Tom, whose appetite had returned with a vengeance in recent weeks, deliberately ate slowly and politely when all he really wanted to do was gorge himself on bread and ladle the soup directly from the pot into his mouth.

The group discussed matters of the day; political and social issues that Tom didn't understand. He listened but did not contribute beyond the occasional strategic nod and smile. Then somebody spoke to him directly. He nearly jumped out of his chair.

"I understand that you are a dab hand when it comes to wood?"

"I wouldn't say that exactly."

"You're too modest, Tom!" exclaimed Theodore. "You've a real talent."

"My wife and I need a new coffee table. Nothing fancy, just something for the living room. We were thinking maybe something in pine."

"Actually I'd prefer cherry," interrupted his wife.

Tom sat open-mouthed, soup dribbling down his chin.

"If you have time, we thought you could come round to the house, have a look, see what you think would look best. We'd pay you, of course."

And so began Tom's career. With Theodore's help, he built them a beautiful coffee table from the finest cherry. It was to be the first of many. The couple, delighted with their purchase, told their friends who in turn told their friends. A fledgling business was born.

Tom lived with Theodore and Margaret for a further six months. He divided his time between his work and his own self-improvement. He enrolled in classes with the local college, basic stuff on literacy and numeracy, for Tom, to his great shame, was barely able to read and write. Theodore helped too, reading *The Times* with him and filling in some of the many gaps in his knowledge along the way. Bit by bit, a whole new world came alive in Tom's mind.

He continued to attend meeting and, after a few weeks, even stood up himself from time to time. He developed an enormous respect for the Quakers, their beliefs and their ideals. The notion of God remained ephemeral, something he occasionally tried to grasp at but could never really get hold of, but his belief in the human spirit, in the love these people had shown him, became a powerful and immovable force in his heart. It formed the bedrock of who he was as he made his way in the world on this, his second coming.

Then the opportunity came to work in Edinburgh. The company was small but renowned for its products: expensive, hand-crafted furniture of the highest quality. There was really no choice to make and Tom accepted on the spot.

He moved into a flat and started a new life on his own. It was difficult at first. He missed the company he'd taken for granted, not to mention the food and comfort he'd enjoyed. The demons grew in strength but the desire to move on, to be a success, kept them at arm's length. He remained on course and off the bottle.

He met Sue shortly after moving to Edinburgh, at Quaker meeting. He was naturally drawn to her but saw no signs of reciprocation nor assumed that there would be any. She was younger than he, educated and from a good family. She had her whole life in front of her and was free from the turmoil and the baggage that Tom's past presented.

At first their conversations were superficial, no more than 'hello, how are you?'. Over the coming weeks, however, their conversations developed and the more they chatted the more Tom warmed to her. He began to think about her during the week and looked forward to seeing her again at the weekend. He began to fall in love.

The idea of reaching out to somebody, of offering his vulnerable self to another, would be like surrendering to the booze all over again. It would also be unfair on her, given how little he had to offer and how much he could potentially take away. He could destroy her and he knew it. And yet the yearning persisted.

Amidst a fit of gargantuan nerves, he asked her if she would like to meet for coffee. To his amazement, she agreed.

When the big day arrived he became feverish, a variety of normally minor irrelevances attaching to themselves a great and unbearable weight in his mind. What should he wear? Should he do something with his hair or leave it be? Should he act casual or serious? And at the root of it all, he worried about his vile, rotten past. He worried and worried and worried until it was too late. Time had stolen a march on him and he hurriedly left the house with a heavy heart and a churning stomach.

They chatted over coffee for more than two hours; the most natural, beautiful and enjoyable two hours of conversation Tom had ever held. During that time, much of his past presented itself naturally. He told her a great many things with frightening ease, as though he were reminding an old friend of things they already knew. She took what he had to say in her stride and, rather than dwell on his past, she accentuated the positives of the new path he was now on. She opened up to him too and shared with him a great many aspects of herself that others would never know. Their meeting was refreshing, fascinating and beyond anything Tom could have hoped for.

For the next two months the couple courted. With neither enjoying great wealth, their encounters were frugal affairs. Edinburgh was enjoying a fine summer and they often strolled together, arm in arm, their hearts entwined, taking in the city's grand architecture and stunning landscape.

Of all the times they spent together, one stood out above all others. They took the bus over to Portobello beach after dinner. It was a warm evening but cloudy and with that strong wind that accompanied most days in the capital. As they walked, ice creams in hand, it began to rain. Not a cold, harsh rain but a warm and gentle summer rain. They gazed out at the sea, which had become excited, the waves thrashing the sand, their hands gripping each other tightly. And then they kissed passionately, the tidal spray washing around their ankles as raindrops showered them from above and the ice creams were surrendered to the sand.

That night they made love for the first time. Tom never imagined that such a simple act could be so intense and so powerful. Nor did he believe he could be so tender with anyone. All the clichés came true.

And the love grew. How it grew! Their bond became stronger and deeper with each passing day, with each warm kiss and heartfelt hug. Tom, introspective as he was, wanted to dance and run and jump and sing and tell the world how great life was. Every day at work he thought of her, and when the day ended he raced home to be lost in her embrace.

The pregnancy was unplanned. Sue had been acting strangely for days and Tom feared that her distance, her preoccupation, signalled a change of heart. He retained a calm exterior but underneath he was readying himself to let go, fearing that she had decided not to be tied down to him and a future together, that he was a mistake she now wanted to rectify.

"We need to talk," she said one evening after dinner.

His heart sunk into the pit of his stomach and he squeaked a painful, mournful reply.

"Sure, what's up?"

There was a pause, painful and drawn out.

"I'm, I mean..."

"What is it? You can tell me." And he reached

out to hold her hand but then stopped himself, scared that the wonder of her touch would be soon be taken from him, that her hand might turn cold and dead when in his.

She shivered as the words left her lips.

"I'm pregnant."

Tom's mind went momentarily blank. It was as though he didn't actually understand what she had said. He repeated them to himself.

"Pregnant. Pregnant?"

And then the fog cleared and the meaning revealed itself.

"PREGNANT!"

And he flung his arms around her, burying his head in her soft, silken hair.

"Oh my darling! I thought you were going to leave me!"

Sue tried to respond but was so choked with tears she couldn't speak.

A new chapter in Tom's resurrection unfolded. The coming of their child brought with it awesome responsibility. The excitement was a nervous, tense excitement. There was the expectancy of new life and of a new life. There was the fear too of complications for Sue and for the child, and deeper fears that he would fail them both, that the now multiplied burden of responsibility would crush him and see him descend back into the wretched darkness. But there was also the determination to succeed, to be a loyal partner to Sue and a great father to their child.

Jessica's arrival was incredible; the culmination of twenty hours of bloody screaming chaos. When it was all over, there she was, wee Jessica, so small and fresh. The moment he saw her, held her in his arms, Tom's life changed forever. Again. He became emboldened with a new and even stronger sense of purpose. Everything he did from now on would be for her. For them.

In the gardens, Tom and Sue found a nice spot of dry grass where few leaves had fallen and spread out an old rug that, many years ago, Sue had lain on as a child in the very same gardens. Tom lay on his back, holding the delighted Jessica above his head so that she floated in the air above him, her inquisitive face beaming back at him. He brought her down onto his chest and then raised her up again, much to her amusement.

"Watch she doesn't burp on you!"

"She'll be fine. Won't you, my dear? Yes, you love flying – wheeeee!"

The sun was now at its apex and, with not a cloud in the sky, covered the city in a vibrant blanket of golden light. The gardens were alive with the chatter of people and wildlife alike, all energised by the sun's brief return in an otherwise dreary and forgettable month.

A dreamy hour or so later the sun finally disappeared behind a grey cloud. Sue gathered up the rug while Tom secured Jessica in the papoose. She had lost interest in her father and with the world in general, having retreated into the peaceful dream world she inhabited for most of the day.

As they packed up and got into the car, Tom considered what to eat for his birthday dinner.

"Maybe a steak." He remarked after some

thought.

"I knew you'd say that! You're so predictable." She grabbed his cheek and pulled on it playfully.

"I know, I know, but I do love steak."

"What do you want with it? Chips, obviously, but what else?"

"Actually," replied Tom, starting the engine. "I was thinking of having mashed potato."

"Oooooh! Maybe I could make gravy?"

"Mmmmm."

"With mushrooms and onions?"

"Mmmmm. Do you mind, I mean? We can have something else."

"Don't be stupid, it's your birthday. And you know I love steak too and we haven't had it for ages."

"True. I think the last time was at your parents."

"That was ages ago, before Jessica was even born!"

"So steak it is. Sirloin."

They had just turned onto Inverleith Row when a sleek black cat decided, at the most inopportune moment, to dart out directly in front of them. Tom instinctively slammed on the brakes and veered out of its way, the car mounting the kerb at right angles to the road. The vehicle behind didn't stand a chance. For a moment time stood still, the passengers freezing in horror as they faced the inevitable. The cars collided in an almighty smash.

Both vehicles lay dormant, the low hum of their engines painfully absent. The tweet of birds could be heard in the trees. The mild breeze continued to rustle leaves and branches. In the distance was the familiar beep of another car horn and voices floated out from nearby houses. Life went on.

Michael and Felicity

The car had taken quite a bump and there was now another large dent to complement the existing ones. The right tail-light was also smashed. The other car, a Volvo estate, had barely a scratch. Its passengers, a couple in their fifties, were shaken but otherwise unharmed.

"I'm terribly sorry," apologised the driver. "That was my fault, I wasn't paying attention."

"Not at all, not at all," insisted Tom. "At least everybody's okay."

The two exchanged insurance details and went their separate ways.

"You should've been paying attention, Michael. Really, that could have been a lot worse," chided his wife Felicity.

"I know, you're right, I'm sorry," responded Michael instinctively.

What he really wanted to say was, 'Maybe I could drive better if you would shut up and let me drive in peace. And if you hadn't forgotten to get carrots yesterday we wouldn't have had to do this at all,' but somehow an apology came out instead.

Sunday, supposedly their day of rest, was anything but, particularly when Felicity was entertaining. She would allow a host of pressures to pile up and then cope by moaning at him. Something would get her started, usually shortly after breakfast, and Michael would bear the brunt of it until the guests arrived, after which he would suffer her exhaustive post-mortem until bed. Experience taught him that when she climbed onto her high horse it was best just to ride it out until she dismounted of her own accord. Today was a day for putting on a smiley-faced mask and shirking all confrontation.

"We'll need to get these carrots par-boiled, along with the potatoes and the other veg, as soon as we get in. Have you taken your stuff out of the kitchen?"

"Your stuff," consisted of a couple of gardening magazines and a sweater, which he had allowed to remain idle on the kitchen table for no more than a few hours.

"Yes, dear, I put them away."

"Sorry, am I being a moan?" asked Felicity, knowing full well that she was.

Michael knew full well what to reply.

"No, no, not at all. I know it's a hassle for you getting everything ready."

Relieved of the burden of guilt, she continued planning and ordering. Michael's mind wandered to tomorrow's meeting. There was a lot to consider, a lot of important issues to discuss. He'd been over every angle a thousand times, had every base covered, but he still feared that something had slipped under his radar. He'd been that way his entire career and this meticulous approach to his work had served him well. Michael was Scotland's chief economist.

Once he'd parked the car in the garage, Felicity was able to inspect the damage at closer quarters. She examined the dent intently, nodded as though wise on such matters, and announced, "Our premiums are definitely going up this year!"

Michael said nothing.

In the kitchen, Felicity busied herself washing and peeling the carrots. Michael was a keen gardener and, in addition to the family garden, which was taken up with flowers and the occasional herb, kept an allotment in Inverleith where he grew an array of vegetables. Handy on days like today when extra were needed, and an invaluable means of escape from the mayhem of family life. But whereas the soil was his domain, the kitchen was very much hers. Michael knew to keep out of her way when she was cooking and retreated to the living room for a well-earned read of the paper.

Before he'd sat down, Hemingway was all over him, barking and slobbering. Michael patted him enthusiastically before directing him to a position at his feet where the dog sat dutifully, staring up at him.

"Sorry, old boy," he remarked, "I've no sweets today."

The basset hound looked back through mournful red eyes.

Felicity had so much to organise and so little time in which to do it. She'd devised a schedule but her error with the carrots had ruined it. The crash had come as a shock too and now she didn't know where she was and mumbled things loudly to herself as she rushed about the room.

When the phone rang she ignored it. Michael did too, waiting for a few rings in the hope that his wife would answer. She didn't and, with Hemingway howling ridiculously as he always did when the phone rang, Michael finally got to his feet and answered it himself.

"Hi, Dad."

The voice at the other end didn't say 'Thank god it's you and not Mum,' but that's exactly what it communicated. It was their elder son, David. He couldn't make it for dinner as he had an essay to do. He was really sorry.

Michael hung up knowing that this would put Felicity in an even worse mood. He was right. He had to hover in the kitchen for several minutes while his wife complained about their son.

He knew when dinner was. He knew how important it was. He knew how much she wanted 'to get the whole family together'. It surely wouldn't have taken much planning and foresight for him to attend? Typical selfish man. Michael replied to his wife at regular intervals, agreeing with whatever she had to say. By the end of their 'conversation', she had decided that David was actually a good son who was, understandably, feeling the pressure of an honours degree at a first class academic institution. Having reached this conclusion, she asked Michael to get out of the kitchen. Michael duly obliged.

The family would descend in less than an hour and the chaos would multiply exponentially. In the meantime, Michael raked leaves in the garden while Hemingway rooted around in the dirt. The sun continued to shine, albeit interrupted by clouds, but there was the feeling of rain to come.

Michael particularly enjoyed mundane gardening tasks such as weeding, trimming or collecting leaves. It was such a mechanical, simple process that his mind could wander freely as he toiled. Invariably it wandered in the direction of work.

Michael and Felicity were both very successful people. Workaholism was therefore unavoidable. Felicity was the director of a cancer charity. The only time when she wasn't working or thinking about work was on Sundays like this when she got herself in a fankle trying to ensure that the potatoes were done and that the meat didn't dry out before the greens were properly steamed.

As a mother and a career woman, Felicity was an expert worrier. To her it wasn't worrying at all, just her normal thought process. There were always things to consider, options to appraise, problems to solve. As she scrubbed the carrots and peeled the potatoes, she mulled over all the family difficulties, all the decisions that would soon have to be made, all the problems that affected her and those close to her. It was the only way she knew how to be.

At present, other than being behind schedule with the cooking, her main worries concerned their younger son, Anthony, who had taken a wrong turn in his life and, at the age of nineteen, was stuck in a dead-end job with no qualifications. Felicity often worried about Anthony but was fast reaching the conclusion that her efforts to help would end in failure and that she'd be better letting go and taking a step back. That was Michael's viewpoint. He believed in a quiet, thoughtful approach, one where he gently guided behind the scenes with an invisible hand. By contrast, Felicity waded in like a war leader, determined to dictate from the front and impose what was right from a position of strength and authority.

At university they were like chalk and cheese, and not even the most talented of clairvoyants would have predicted their future life together. Felicity was a real livewire. Passionate, determined and never afraid to make waves, she always made her opinions heard. Hers was a bullish character, confrontational and unwilling to budge an inch on her left-wing principles.

Michael was completely the opposite. He was a pragmatist who looked at issues from a number of different sides. It was often unclear what, if anything, he actually thought about a topic, and at university he played devil's advocate in discussions, playing arguments and ideas against each other.

Michael was always going to join the establishment. His family were conservative with a small 'c' and his upbringing was a grounded one. To everyone at university it was obvious that he would become a grey suited civil servant.

Felicity was more likely to end up on a picket line or in a commune. Her upbringing had been as equally benign as Michael's – respectable family, good school, a home life dictated by religious conservatism – yet her reaction to it couldn't have been more different. She hated the old racist, sexist political structures that bound the island and was determined to break them. In her first year she flirted with revolutionary communism. Michael joined the chess club.

Michael didn't know Felicity in those days but he knew of her and he would be lying if he didn't admit that from the beginning he found her attractive. Not a strong feeling, more of a recognition within himself every time he saw her. She had a spark about her and great intelligence too, and he couldn't help but admire her in his own quiet way.

They didn't meet properly until third year, at a mutual friend's party. The calamitous Vietnam War was at its height and Felicity, surrounded by sycophantic and less able friends always happy to support her views, let rip on what she thought of the imperialists who were 'massacring the poor in pursuit of their own self-enrichment'.

Michael listened to her for a while without saying anything. She loved the sound of her own voice and had that great intellectual ability to talk exhaustively about something without ever contradicting herself or sounding, even for a brief moment, as though she possessed anything less than a completely authoritative grasp of the subject. This impressed Michael greatly, her socialist rhetoric less so.

"The war in Vietnam has undoubtedly been a military disaster for the Americans," he finally replied coolly. "However, given the geopolitical importance of the region and the activities of the Soviet Union and China, I can entirely understand why Kennedy and then Johnson both felt the need to intervene. It's difficult to say what the political landscape would look like had the USA stepped back in '65 but I can't imagine it looking any better. The United States has made many errors in Vietnam and elsewhere but I don't believe the Soviets have behaved in a manner that should be applauded. Nor do I regard theirs or China's system of government, which they are seeking to impose on Vietnam, to be preferable to the one Washington is fighting for."

They ended up being the last two people to leave the party, having argued politics all evening. They didn't speak again for a few weeks, then met by chance in a pub. Again they argued vociferously, this time on the situation in Northern Ireland. Again they were the last people to leave.

Felicity spoke to Michael with an air of contempt and showed no signs that she found him attractive or even that she liked him at all. Her tone was harsh, her language laced with spiteful jibes and personal insults. Michael was his usual measured self and did not allow himself to get angry or flustered but rather offered his sound arguments to her very calmly and sensibly, something which annoyed her no end.

They occasionally met at parties or other social gatherings in the following months, or just around campus. They generally discussed something or other and rarely agreed. There was no hint of romance.

It was in the summer that the sparring turned into something more. Michael needed to earn money to pay his rent and found himself a job in a bookshop, serving customers and ensuring the books were presented appropriately on the shelves. One afternoon Felicity came in to browse.

On seeing Michael she explained, "I'm looking for an improving book."

"Oh come now, Felicity, you don't need improving!" Not only did Felicity laugh, she smiled directly at him, her eyes sparkling brightly. This was no ordinary smile like the one she would flash his way after she'd said something particularly smart or insulting. This was an altogether different smile and for the next few days Michael thought about what it meant and how he should respond to it.

When he met her again, this time by chance in the biscuit aisle of the Co-Op, he took the initiative and asked her out. Thirty years and three children later they were still together.

Their union hadn't been without its ups and downs. Felicity could be a difficult person most of the time, somebody who was always sure that she knew best. In the first two years that they co-habited, above an antiques shop in Causewayside, arguments were frequent and exhausting, generally ending in the bedroom, which in turn led to a young family and all the fun and chaos that entailed.

Having come to terms with both the belated preparations for the meal and the absence of her elder son, Felicity was now in a better frame of mind and was making good progress readying the vegetables. She briefly stopped what she was doing and went into the garden where she wrapped her arms around her husband and whispered "Sorry for being such a moan". He responded with a kiss, his heart as giddy as it ever was when she held him.

Felicity returned indoors to check on the meat, which was roasting nicely, the inviting smell of the beef filling the kitchen as soon as she opened the oven door. It was to be a standard British Sunday lunch, or rather late lunch. Roast beef and all the trimmings. Felicity, inspired by the explosion of television cookery shows, had wanted to try something different and imaginative. She had a recipe for Cajun roast beef and dreamed of serving spiced-up Silverside with creamy mashed potatoes and corn on the cob grilled until the kernels were on the cusp of burning.

Her mother, however, was very particular when it came to food and even more particular when it came to roast beef. She was in her late seventies and from that meat-and-two-veg generation that liked their food bland and spice-free. Felicity knew that one day her mother would no longer be able to come for Sunday lunch and so continued to keep the meal simple on these occasions. She did, however, allow herself the luxury of roasting some garlic and red onions, something her mother didn't approve of.

Felicity was straining the par-boiled carrots and potatoes when Anthony arrived. He had been playing football and glistened with sweat, his knees caked in mud.

"Hi son, how was your game?"

"Alright," he grunted, before grabbing a banana from the fruit bowl and heading straight for his bedroom.

From her position in the kitchen, she could see Michael busying around in the garden, Hemingway running around him excitedly. He was always so engrossed in his gardening, so focused. In his dark brown eyes she could see the same intensity and quiet determination she fell in love with all those years ago. Whenever she saw that look she instinctively wanted to grab him and make love. But with their son in the house and the rest of the family on their way, she contented herself with a smile that nobody else would see.

Despite the carrot-run and the shock of the crash, Felicity had managed to get everything ready on time and the meat was resting when the doorbell rang. She opened the door to find a beautiful little face beaming up at her.

"Hi, Granny!"

"Hiya, sweetheart!" and she patted the child warmly on the head, ruffling her golden curls as she did so.

"How are you?"

"I'm great! Daddy took me for a bike ride this morning. I don't need stabilisers anymore, I can ride all by myself!"

"Well done Anna!"

Following along behind, carrying a bottle of wine, was Felicity's daughter Jennifer. She had the same fair hair as Anna and the same big blue eyes. Felicity couldn't help thinking how much Anna reminded her of Jennifer when she was a child; so energetic and full of wonder.

Helping Felicity's mother out of the car was Jennifer's husband George and, having warmly embraced her daughter, Felicity rushed to greet them.

"Hi Mum, are you okay?"

Despite being the undisputed ruler of the household and a generally imposing and confident figure, Felicity always sounded meek and subservient when addressing her mother.

"Yes, yes, I'm fine," she replied, flustered by all the attention.

Michael came in from the garden, greeting his grand-daughter and daughter with affectionate hugs and George with a firm handshake. He gave his mother-in-law a curt nod.

190

In the living room, which was grand and airy, much in keeping with what was a fine old house, little Anna effortlessly took centre-stage as the rest of the family doted on her.

"Granny, Granny, put Aretha on, put Aretha on!"

"In a minute, sweetheart, just let Granny get everybody drinks first."

"Surely we're going to be spared that for once?" remarked Anthony who was washed and presentable and as amiable and good-natured as anyone would ever encounter him. The presence of his grandmother had that effect.

Anna was a bold and excitable girl who loved to sing and dance, very much as her mother did as a child. When she was very young, Jennifer would sing along to her mother's Aretha Franklin records, usually with a hairbrush or some other prop serving as a microphone. This tradition had continued and Anna sang and danced to the same songs, her mother providing backing vocals. On occasions such as these, and with the men of the family shaking their heads, three generations of women would belt out R-E-S-P-E-C-T complete with swaying hips and gliding hands. Catherine didn't join in but approved all the same, always remarking that musical talent ran through her mother's side of the family. She would then ramble on about one or other of her aunts or cousins who had performed in Paris or in London or had sung with distinction for the local church choir.

Felicity played the hostess more with fear than finesse. Her desire to please everybody, to get everything right, meant she dashed around, fussing and occasionally tutting to herself.

"Your father and I had a prang today," explained Felicity as she brought through a tray of drinks.

Michael looked crestfallen.

"My word, what happened?"

Michael swooped in before his wife had a chance to answer.

"The car in front swerved. I should have braked sooner. I wasn't paying enough attention."

"Was anybody hurt?"

"No, no, just a wee dent."

"It was a young couple," continued Felicity. "They had a baby too, really young. They were quite shaken up by it."

"Typical male driver!" remarked Catherine, casting a glare in the direction of Michael. "Always driving fast and recklessly."

"What's a prang, mummy?"

"It's when two cars bang into each other."

"Why would they do that?"

"They don't mean it, they just sometimes do it by accident."

"Does it hurt the cars when they do that?"

Anthony chuckled.

"No, sweetie," explained her father. "Cars are very, very strong."

The meal was a veritable feast, the table expressing a communal lick of the lips as hot plates arrived from the kitchen. The beef, expertly carved by Michael, took pride of place. Scattered around it were dozens of roast potatoes, carrots and parsnips that glistened a golden caramel. The onions and garlic were also nestled in beside them, giving off a beautifully sweet smell that contrasted with the richness of the meat. Other dishes contained steamed carrots and broccoli, peas, mashed potatoes, and giant Yorkshire puddings that overflowed from their tray. Dark gravy floated in a large boat and several pots of horseradish and mustard dotted the table.

"This is wonderful Mum!"

"Absolutely fantastic!" agreed George who was already passing round the warmed plates.

Silence descended on the table as everyone got stuck in. Anthony piled his plate high with meat, potatoes and Yorkshires, liberally pouring gravy over them. Anna, whose taste buds were not well developed and was a fussy eater, went for the mashed potatoes with a little bit of beef which her father dutifully cut into bite-sized pieces. This brought a look of disdain from Catherine.

"You really should make her eat some greens."

The others paid no attention.

Felicity and her daughter, who were both health conscience and semi-vegetarian, piled their plates with steamed vegetables, taking only a little meat. Catherine took a little of everything save the roasted onions and garlic, commenting that they never ate such things in her day. George and Michael took a lot of everything. The table was awash with smiles and compliments, everybody enjoying the excellent home-cooked food.

"Fantastic Yorkshires! How do you get them to rise so well?"

"That's a secret I share with Delia!"

"I love the red onions – so sweet."

"They go great with the beef."

"Mmmmm, the garlic's lovely too."

Even Catherine had to admit that the beef was 'delightful' and, for a change, made no remark about it tasting better in her day. Predictably, however, she remarked that the vegetables were underdone. Felicity and her siblings had all grown up hating vegetables and it was only when she visited the house of a Chinese friend at university that she discovered the joys of steamed vegetables, which were packed with flavour and still retained their bite.

"How's the decorating going, George?"

George seemed surprised by his mother-in-law's question and stopped in mid-bite, a large piece of meat hanging awkwardly from his mouth as he turned to his wife. She looked equally confused.

"Decorating? Oh yes, of course, the kitchen. Slowly!" And she produced a confused frown.

This set alarm bells ringing for Felicity. She'd noticed Jennifer being slightly apprehensive when she arrived. This brief and seemingly innocent exchange was the corroboration. Her mother's instinct knew that something was wrong.

Jennifer met George whilst still at university and, much to her parents' disappointment, became pregnant before she finished her course. Felicity, who had always extolled the virtues of being an independent and educated woman, was particularly upset. George was not the son-in-law she'd had in mind either. Like all mothers, she imagined that her daughter would marry somebody handsome, charming and wildly successful. George was an average sort of man, pleasant and good natured if somewhat gormless. His future would very definitely be middle-of-the-road.

To George's credit, however, he stuck by Jennifer when many men would have run a mile. He found work, they married, moved into a rundown flat and struggled as young families do. When Anna got a bit older, Jennifer went back to university and finished her course. She was now working and the family were doing well and making a fine job of raising Anna, who was everything Felicity had hoped for in a grand-daughter.

Perhaps the strain was getting to them. Perhaps that, having got together at such a young age, they now wanted to go their separate ways. Perhaps he'd had an affair. These thoughts troubled Felicity as she served up dessert, her face all smiles but her head and heart quite the opposite.

"Rhubarb crumble and custard – fantastic! You sure know how to spoil us, Felicity," remarked George.

"Is the rhubarb from the allotment?" asked Jennifer.

"Yes, grown by your father's own fair hands."

"Well I hope you waited until it was properly ripe," commented Catherine.

He had, and this quintessential British classic proved a fitting end to a wonderful meal.

Before Felicity had a chance to take away the plates, all of which were thoroughly clean, Jennifer tapped on her glass with a fork and said that she had an announcement to make.

Felicity's heart sank yet the smile on her

daughter's face did not indicate that they were about to announce their divorce. For a brief moment Felicity felt confused, out of control, something she was neither used to nor enjoyed.

"What on earth is it?" Her thoughts flew off her tongue without her realising and she was taken back by her own abruptness.

"Well, you see, George and I. Well, I mean…"

Everyone at the table looked perplexed save George and little Anna who smiled smugly.

"They're moving away," thought Felicity. That must be it. George had always had a thing about Australia. He must have found a job there and would be taking her only daughter and grand-daughter with him. She'd barely see them, maybe the odd Christmas if she were lucky. Anna would grow up through photos and video clips until, one day, her and Michael would fly half way round the world to the wedding of a woman they barely knew.

This had happened to her colleague. Her son met an American girl and emigrated to Chicago just a year after finishing school. She never saw him and struggled to save the money to visit. Australia was even further away, a more expensive, more tiring journey. The other side of the world.

Felicity's face drooped as her mind descended on this sad thought. Then her daughter spoke.

"We're expecting a new addition. Another child!"

Felicity was struck by a powerful sense of relief and nearly blurted out "Oh thank God!" Catherine produced one of her only genuine smiles of the afternoon and even the normally sullen Anthony seemed pleased. Michael was over the moon and immediately rushed to the wine rack for a bottle of Dom Perignon he'd been saving for a special occasion.

"So I'm going to have two great-grandchildren!" exclaimed Catherine delightedly. "My, my."

"I can't believe it," said Felicity. "I knew something was up but I didn't know what. And did you know all along?" she asked Anna.

The child grinned and nodded.

"I promised Mummy I wouldn't tell anyone."

The spent the remainder of the afternoon in the living room where the family played charades, sang songs and rooted through old family albums. Michael sat in his favourite chair, Hemingway nestled by his feet. He watched little Anna laugh and play, and thought of the next arrival and the joy it would bring.

He loved being a grandfather; all the pleasures of fatherhood but few of the worries. He was able to take a step back and watch her grow up from a safe distance. He felt great pride that the love he and Felicity had found should grow into this. Theirs was an excellent life and one they would continue to enjoy for many years to come.

Anthony

As soon as his relatives left, Anthony disappeared upstairs to his room where he switched on his computer. This was where he spent most of his free time, alone in virtual reality. Here he could escape the relentless unhappiness that characterised his young life. Yet with each day he spent alone in his room, he distanced himself that little bit further from the rest of the world, from his friends and his family, and from a promising and happy life.

Anthony hated his life on several fronts, not least his occupation. Or lack of. He had been working as a temp for over a year now, permanent jobs being like gold-dust, companies preferring casual labour they could sack on a whim.

Temporary employment was wretched purgatory. No future and no security. The work was mind-numbingly repetitive. Low paid. Morale-sapping. He behaved extra well. Worked extra hard. Mornings. Nights. Weekends. Whatever his lord and master desired. Smiling through gritted teeth as morons ordered him to do this and do that. He was at the bottom but that didn't mean he couldn't fall any lower.

And so, early tomorrow morning he would dust himself down, iron out the anger as best he could, for some creases always remained, and run to the bus-stop, his heart pounding all the way for fear he might miss it. Five excruciatingly long days would pass, minute by agonising minute, until the weekend reared its head with empty promises of fun and adventure, only to slap him in the face with the reminder that he'd already blown it.

On a Sunday evening, with the clock racing towards bedtime, the thought of Monday sent a shiver down Anthony's spine. With each passing minute the knot in his stomach tightened. All day he processed the accounts of people far wealthier and successful than he. Shuffling paper, clicking his mouse, running to the photocopier. Over and over and over again. That was the week that lay ahead.

Perhaps it would be better if he enjoyed the company of the people he worked with. He didn't. Most of them were idiots, so ignorant they couldn't even spell the word. Racist, sexist, homophobic morons. And yet infinitely better than he, the useless temp who couldn't even find a real job. Some of the comments his colleagues spouted made him feel physically sick. Sick that he'd allowed himself no option but to be in their company. Every day was tabloid ignorance.

"I can't believe they let these people in. All they do is steal and scrounge off the state."

And then there was his supervisor. A bitter, horrible man who took delight in the power he held over junior colleagues. He was also lazy to the point of uselessness and hideously incompetent. Anthony had spent all day Friday photocopying documents only to find that another colleague had already done them. His supervisor had given him the instruction and yet Anthony knew he would somehow get the blame for this duplication of effort, which he would accept meekly and without complaint.

There was just one person in his office he got on with. A young guy called Danny who was witty and never stopped complaining about their co-workers. He was merely on a job outing, however, having taken a year out from his studies to 'write a novel'. He had no cares and no worries. Soon he would find a better job, a job Anthony could never dream of getting, and he'd be off.

Most temps were the same. They were either students earning extra cash or foreigners on holiday. Either way they didn't care. They were free to pick and choose, their job merely a brief sojourn from a far more interesting reality. For Anthony this was his life. This was, he feared, as good as it was going to get.

None of the girls in the office gave him a second glance. To them he was just a skivvy. No money and no talent. With every day that they ignored him he became more resentful. More spiteful.

Anthony was also weighed down by the enormous expectation placed on him by his family. It was unwritten, unmentioned almost, but it loomed over him all the same. His parents were frighteningly successful, as were his aunts, uncles and cousins. Every family update revolved around a promotion or other successful endeavour. Most of these updates were also, however, laced with an undercurrent of perceived middle class morality. This made it even harder. Anthony was expected to be an outstanding success, but only within a narrowly defined sphere of what his parents, in particular his mother, considered acceptable.

"Your cousin Brian got his exam results back – a first class honours with distinction from Oxford. He's been offered a job in the City. With some bank or other. Big money. Working for the man. Makes me sick to think of his talents being used in such a wicked way!"

"Auntie Pauline has just been made Deputy Head of Amnesty International. She will be even busier than she already is – if that were possible! I can see her next move being into the UN. She certainly has the language skills, speaks five already and is now learning Mandarin. It's great to see her doing so well, she works really hard."

Then there was his brother David; the apple of his mother's eye, always that bit better at everything than he, and now meeting the family's expectations of studying for an honours degree at university. Anthony, who had singularly failed to meet this baseline requirement, felt like the black sheep of the family by comparison. The failure.

He thought of Mary Green. Her beautiful blue eyes thrust another dagger into him. Mary Green. Mary Green. Mary fucking Green. The most beautiful girl in school. The first girl he'd ever loved. The girl he'd failed to get, being too awkward and shy a teenager to make the move she had wanted him to. Mary continued to exist inside his head and heart as a haunting memory. As a reminder of his failure. He occasionally saw her on nights out. Always when he least expected to and was least ready to cope. She would approach him all smiles and chat to him as she always did. Like he was a girlfriend. She would tell him personal things he did not wish to hear. More anguish to tuck away. More twists of the knife embedded in his heart. More sleepless nights. Seven long years after he'd fallen for her smile.

Last night was one of those nights. He'd been out with friends and was considerably the worse for wear when she appeared out of nowhere, hugging him warmly and tearing him apart with those big blue eyes. He tried to remain composed as she described her latest boyfriend, fighting back the urge to break down and cry in front of her. He left the club immediately, sobbing all the way home.

He was sure that if only he'd had the guts to ask Mary Green out all those years ago, if only he'd taken the plunge and put his pride on the line, he'd be happy now. He'd be a different person. The experience and the happiness she would have provided would have set him on a different path. A better path. He'd be a confident young man instead of the pathetic wretch he faced each and every morning. If only he'd told her then how he felt his life now would be wonderful. He dreamt that one day he would get the chance to tell her and that the impossible would occur. That his current nightmare was part of a beautiful and as yet incomplete love story. Deep down, however, he knew that his desire was no more than a warped adolescent infatuation based on a person who didn't actually exist but merely inhabited in his mind Mary Green's perfect body. He thought about sex constantly. With her.

No matter how hard he tried, Anthony was unable to slow down the maelstrom in his mind. With each lonely day he became more desperate and more disturbed. He felt imprisoned. Trapped in a life that was not of his choosing. It constricted him so that he couldn't breathe. And then most unexpectedly the fog would lift and he would experience a strange sense of euphoria. He was always one or the other. There was no balance.

How long had he felt like this? These feelings certainly preceded Mary Green and the trials of adolescence. Anthony could recall as a young child believing that he was evil, that everybody hated him, and that if he told anybody he would be taken away and locked up. Self-hatred and rage were the first memories he could recall. Perhaps they had developed in his sub-conscious as a baby. Maybe even in the womb. He thought about this endlessly as his brain spun

round

and round   and round

and round   and round

and round   and round

and round

faster and faster and faster and faster it would turn until he thought he would explode.

Was this normal? Others, not least his mother, thought not and had urged him to seek help. To that end he had visited a psychiatrist. £300 an hour of his parents' money to be told he did not have a mental illness. That his problems were 'behavioural'. What did that even mean?

Then there was his previous GP. He

recommended Depixol, an anti-psychotic drug, With little feeling or emotion he explained that they would inject this into Anthony's posterior once a month, that it would cause 'weight gain and sexual dysfunctionalism'. Anthony had run a mile.

There was chink of light, however. Far off but still visible. Anthony had seen another GP recently about his asthma. During the discussions they got onto his moods and the doctor casually floated the idea that Anthony had low levels of serotonin on the brain and that a particular drug could restore those levels to normal.

"It has several names but most people know it as Prozac. It isn't like people think, doesn't drug you up and isn't addictive. It just helps the brain to function as it should."

The thought of taking medication frightened Anthony. But at the same time the thought that what he was going through actually was a medical condition, and that there was a cure, gave him hope. The doctor had given him a form to fill in. Something called a HAD sheet with sad and smiley faces. He would get round to filling it in next week.

It was late now. Time to sleep. Monday beckoned. Anthony forlornly shut down his computer and crawled into bed, wrapping the covers tightly around him as though they were a woman's arms. He imagined being in love and being loved. Of being happy. As the night drew to a close he thought of Mary Green too, as he always did, the satisfaction tinged with bitter, suicidal regret.

Monday

Epilogue

With Monday came the cold, harsh reality of another week. Weary souls rubbed the sleep from their eyes with a feeling of dread in their stomach and a bitter resignation in their hearts. Work was an inevitability for most, the weekend having been painfully short and unfulfilling. For every high there was a low and they didn't get much lower than Monday morning.

By seven o'clock everyone in the Taylor household was up and ready for the new week. Everyone except Anthony. He had this remarkable ability to sleep right through his radio alarm clock. All the loud music did was influence the bizarre dream he experienced immediately prior to his mother shaking him awake. This morning she was in a rush and in no mood to entertain coming upstairs.

"Anthony! Anthony, its gone seven, time to get up!"

She had been doing this for over a decade. Every single day. And every day he ignored her.

By ten past seven frustration got the better of her and she stormed upstairs in a whirlwind of fury. She burst in on her idle son, sprawled unconscious across the bed, the bedclothes lying discarded on the floor.

"Anthony! Anthony!"

He didn't move. Not at all.

"Anthony! Get up!"

She shook him aggressively but still he showed no signs of life.

"Every bloody day it's the same with you!"

This time there was a slight stir, no more than a

murmur and a momentary shake of the head.

"It's time to get up. You have to go to work."

These were the first words of the week that Anthony would hear. He mumbled something, his stupefied face souring with the displeasure of it all. He had to go to work. He had to. Go to. Work.

"Bastard!" and his eyes shot open.

"Language!"

As he crawled out of bed his mother explained, "I'm going to Glasgow this morning. I haven't had time to cook you breakfast," her voice faltering as though she had somehow failed him, "but there's some toast out and plenty of cereal."

"Okay."

On the floor was a pile of dirty clothes that his mother glanced at scornfully. On top of the pile was his distinctive red shirt, still stinking of alcohol and tobacco from the nightclub he'd been to on Saturday night. She had bought it for him in Paris. It was too good a shirt to be tossed carelessly on the floor and she immediately delivered it to the washing machine.

Anthony thought briefly of Friday's tryst and felt a swelling down below. But that sense of enjoyment was soon replaced by shame, and of guilt over the money he'd squandered. He was no longer a virgin and yet he could share this fact with no one, meaning he really was still a virgin. Having thought of losing his virginity with Mary Green every day for year, the fact that he had lost it with a prostitute made him sick.

He pulled on his dressing gown and headed for the kitchen, his face a scowl and his mind ablaze with ugly thoughts. Mr Taylor was sitting at the breakfast table, a broadsheet shielding his bespectacled face from view. He mumbled a greeting but did not stir from his earnest reading. Anthony muttered likewise and seated himself. As he picked up a slice of toast his instant reaction was "Mum, this toast is cold," to which his father promptly replied, "Make it yourself then," again without looking up.

But his wife was already in mother mode and put some more on apologetically as Anthony helped himself to cereal.

"We'll have to contact the insurers today, Michael."

"You're right. I'll get onto it as soon as I get to work. Do you have the contact details?"

"Yes, sure, they're in my handbag," and she rushed through to get them. She hadn't stopped rushing around since she got up.

Anthony was mildly interested in finding out more about this car crash they had been involved in, and the protagonist they had run into, but only so that he could make unhelpful comments that wouldn't go down well at all. But whatever it was that stopped him talking to his parents most of the time, except when he wanted something, stopped him doing so here. The words could be on the tip of his tongue and yet some infuriating mechanism within him refused them to be released. Most days he couldn't even say hello. The phrase just got stuck somewhere in his throat and came out as an angry snarl.

His mother returned with a folded piece of paper,

which she handed to her husband.

"I think his name was Richards. Something like that."

Mr Taylor put down his newspaper and unfolded the piece of paper.

"That's right, Richards. Tom Richards. Sounded like he was from The Midlands, somewhere like that."

Miss Richards was working today, unaware that her father lived a stone's throw from the massage parlour. On her way she popped into Mr Palavar's shop to buy cigarettes. He was his usual cheery self.

Michael deposited the piece of paper into his trouser pocket and returned to the morning's news. There was always a business-like air to Mr Taylor in the mornings, a dour seriousness that he was unable to shake off until shortly before bed most weeknights.

Before his father had a chance, Anthony snatched the newspaper from the table.

"Hey, I was reading that!"

"I'll just be a second, just want to know what's going on in the world."

The world had, as always, delivered its quota of war, disease, famine and scandal. And a brutal murder had been committed in the capital in the early hours of Saturday morning. A nineteen year old man had been beaten to death. An Irish taxi driver was in custody. Two officers had been injured during his arrest.

Three slices of toast and a shower later, Anthony pulled on his office attire, fumbling to button his shirt in a hurry and cursing the tight fit of his trousers.

He hadn't shaved and had no intention of doing so, as was the case every morning, until that nagging voice told him that other people would look badly upon him if he arrived unshaven. Even though it was no more than a smattering of stubble it was enough to label him scruffy and unprofessional. Cursing this rotten misfortune, and the march of time, he scraped it off in anguish, his skin threatening to peel and split under the pressure. A shaving cut was all he needed. Thankfully his face stayed intact and he burst out of the house with dabs of shaving foam still hanging from his chin, knowing only too well he didn't have enough time to get to work before nine.

He could see his bus just ahead of him. It was at the lights and with pace and some providence he might just make it. He started to sprint. The lights remained at red, the traffic static as he pulled up alongside, his feet already burning and swollen. Then the lights turned green and the bus left him behind. The bus stop was a good hundred metres away and Anthony was no athlete. He covered the distance faster than he had ever done previously, a new personal best, but it still wasn't enough. As he stopped to catch his breath the bus had already moved off. The driver must have been in charitable mood, however, as he stopped a few metres further up.

"It's your lucky day, son!"

"Cheers, mate," he said to the driver, his cheeks flushed and his fringe damp with sweat.

"Nae bother. Bet you thought you were gonna be

late for work?"

"Aye," he replied, now wishing he'd called in sick.

The bus was full to bursting with frustrated commuters jostling for position. Anthony squeezed his way into a space, carefully avoiding the elbows and umbrellas that protruded in all directions. It was stiflingly warm, the close proximity of so many bodies creating a horrible, close atmosphere. As the bus lurched so did the mass of people, swaying from side to side, faces contorted with anguish.

As he deliberated over The Wu Tang Clan or Stone Roses, the battery on his CD player went dead. Rain spat off the windows. It was light at first but soon became heavy, turning the city grey and desolate. Puddles quickly formed in the gutters and on the uneven pavements, producing thick, dirty pools of litter-infested soup. The wind began to howl.

Anthony thought of his brother David. He wouldn't be awake until noon, unless he was still up on a weekend binge. Either way, the supposedly diligent student wouldn't be anywhere near a lecture theatre today. Or any other day for that matter. To think his parents honestly believed he couldn't make Sunday lunch because he was studying! Anthony had wanted to tell them the truth about their golden boy so many times. But he never did.

David Taylor was indeed still in bed after a heavy weekend. Rebecca, on the other hand, was already on her way to the library and was thinking of the young man in the distinctive red shirt.

The traffic was thick and painfully slow.

Anthony's heart was beating fast and his stomach ached with dread. He was going to be late. This was now an inevitability. He had done this journey enough times before to realise that. There was no cheating the grinding traffic.

He had already been late several times recently. He just couldn't motivate himself to get up any earlier, to get out of the house that little bit sooner. The only drive he had was fear. The perennial taskmaster. The same reason everyone else was on this bus. Being late, even by a minute, would result in a ticking-off. And boy did his supervisor know how to give those.

He tried desperately to recall how many times he had been late. How many times he had been criticised for failing to complete a task or for making a mistake. How many times the boss had shaken his head disdainfully in his direction. How many times he had caused irritation by asking the obvious. How many minutes he had wasted going to the canteen or to the toilet. How much precious profit he had lost the company. How close he was to the sack.

"Hey Tony, how are you?" came an unfamiliar voice.

Anthony looked up, startled.

"Alright."

"Jimmy. We used to work together at the bank."

"I'm still there," replied Anthony in utter resignation.

"Yeah?" Jimmy's eyes were full of sympathy.

Anthony remembered him now. He had sat a few desks away from him when he first started. He was a funny guy, full of amusing anecdotes. He also took no shit from the bosses, something Anthony respected. He did no work either and Anthony presumed he'd been sacked.

"Where are you now?"

"I'm out at Saughton House, working for the government." He said the last part as though he were a spy or some high-ranking scientist working on secret military projects.

"Doing what?"

"Absolutely fuck all, mate!"

"Sounds good."

"It's great. Really. When I get in, and it doesn't matter what time cos I'm on flexi, I'll head straight for the canteen, pick up a paper and a couple of bacon rolls, relax. That's what everybody does. It's a total skive."

"What's the money like?"

"About the same as the bank."

"Sounds great!"

"You should give the agency a call. They're always looking for temps. Here, I think I've got a card," and he rummaged in his pockets.

"Here you go. Give them a call today and they'll have you a job in no time. You could be out of the bank within a week."

"That's quality, cheers!"

Anthony felt energised by this new information. Here was an opportunity to get away from the bank, to get away from his wretched job and his bastard boss and start again somewhere else. Somewhere better. He would call the agency at lunchtime. Definitely.

The bus somehow made up time and Anthony

was able to show his pass to the dour security guard with a full minute to spare. For once his boss wouldn't be able to say anything.

There was an atmosphere in the office. Anthony noticed it as soon as he came in. People weren't themselves. They spoke in hushed whispers. His heart sank. He could feel the axe hanging over him. Maybe the team was being wound up. Perhaps the whole operation was being relocated to China as part of some rationalisation exercise. And perhaps the promises of a government job would prove empty. It was all going horribly wrong.

He tried to catch someone's eye, to have somebody confirm or assuage his fear. But everybody blanked him and he switched on his computer wondering if he'd even get the chance to use it. Then there was a tap on his shoulder. It was Danny, who beckoned him to follow him over to the photocopier and away from the other people in the office.

Once they were a safe distance away he whispered, "Have you heard the news?"

"Nope, what's going on?"

Danny looked around the room before directing Anthony even further away, to the sanctuary of the vending machine in the corridor outside. He appeared both excited and nervous. Anthony could only ever remember Danny behaving with complete indifference before. This was all very peculiar.

"You'll not have to worry about the boss anymore," said Danny in a low whisper.

"How, did the fat cunt get the sack?"

"Nah, he's dead! Heart attack. Rumour is – but

you never heard this from me – he came home on Saturday night and found his wife in bed with another man! Dropped dead right there and then."

Lee was already in the gym working up a sweat. The married woman he'd seduced on Saturday hadn't been back in touch. He had another date lined up anyway. A young mum whose husband worked on the rigs.

Anthony paused for a second before speaking, thoughtfully weighing up his words. Glancing out of the window he could see sunlight breaking through the grey clouds. He turned to Danny and replied "Poor James Urquhart." By the time he got back to his desk he was already looking forward to next weekend.

Acknowledgements

A massive thank you for all their help and inspiration goes to David Rice, Gordon Lawrie, Emma Baird, Natalie Schupfer, Joseph White, Euan Johnstone, Stephane Adam, John Mulligan, Robert Louis Stevenson, My Mum, Nuw Idol, Lizzie Beattie, Irvine Welsh, Kerrin Clapton, John Robertson, Emile Zola, Janet and Jerry, Nicola McGhee, Robert Fitzgerald Diggs, Kevin MacNeil, Chenjurin, Mikhail Lermontov, Paulina Makles, Ann Budge, John Mulligan, DJ Hype, Salman Rushdie and Eva Rehse.

About Comely Bank Publishing

Comely Bank Publishing (CBP) is a co-operative publishing house giving bright, new talent a platform.

Founded in 2012, CBP aims to tackle the quality issues faced by traditional publishing, i.e. the concentration on books only by established authors or bankable names. CPB helps new authors publish at low cost and makes no profits from its authors.

Comedy, historical fiction, young adult fiction and more – Comely Bank Publishing covers many genres and we are sure you will find a book you enjoy…

All books are available in print and ebook formats on Amazon, Kobo and other outlets, as well as in Edinburgh bookshops and directly from the Comely Bank Publishing website, www.comelybankpublishing.com.

FOUR OLD GEEZERS AND A VALKYRIE
Gordon Lawrie

Four Old Geezers and a Valkyrie by Gordon Lawrie is an entertaining romp set in contemporary Edinburgh. Brian, aka 'Captain', is a recently-retired, disillusioned teacher who has split acrimoniously with his wife. A chance meeting with his best man encourages Captain to dig out his 40-year-old guitar which leads to a series of hilarious jam sessions. Posting the results on YouTube, they prove to be surprise hits…

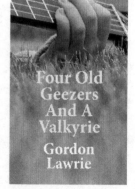